"THERE MUST BE MAG[...]
SAID. BUT HOW? V[...]
THAT HOW SHE WAS CONTROLLING THESE WOMEN?

The door opened before they'd even had a chance to touch it. This time, though, they weren't met by a single, business suit–clad woman, but by four tall, muscular women dressed in pink sports bras, jogging shorts, and sneakers. Looking at their powerful physiques—broad shoulders, massive upper arms, corded thighs—Paige felt very small.

Phoebe could take them, Paige thought. Between her martial arts skills and her levitation powers, even four Amazons didn't stand a chance. And these weren't real Amazons anyway, just figurative Amazons. She noticed that Phoebe had tensed, and believed her sister was probably weighing the odds as well. The women were smiling at them, but the mood had changed. Confrontation was in the air.

"Ms. Winship is ready to see you now," one of them announced.

Charmed®

Published by Simon & Schuster

SURVIVAL OF THE FITTEST

An original novel by Jeff Mariotte

Based on the hit TV series created by

Constance M. Burge

SIMON SPOTLIGHT ENTERTAINMENT
New York   London   Toronto   Sydney

To Maryelizabeth, who enchants me

This book is a work of fiction. Any references to historical events, real people, or real locales are used fictitiously. Other names, characters, places, and incidents are the product of the author's imagination, and any resemblance to actual events or locales or persons, living or dead, is entirely coincidental.

S|S|E

SIMON SPOTLIGHT ENTERTAINMENT
An imprint of Simon & Schuster Children's Publishing Division
1230 Avenue of the Americas, New York, New York 10020
® & © 2004 Spelling Television Inc. All Rights Reserved.
All rights reserved, including the right of reproduction in whole or in part in any form.
SIMON SPOTLIGHT ENTERTAINMENT and related logo are trademarks of Simon & Schuster, Inc.
Manufactured in the United States of America
First Edition 10 9 8 7 6 5 4 3 2 1
Library of Congress Control Number 2004102533
ISBN 0-689-86852-9

SURVIVAL OF
THE FITTEST

Prologue

Marianne and Kevin Haas had been married for four years but home owners for just under four weeks. Their new home, a turquoise with yellow trim row house, was three blocks from Golden Gate Park, had three bedrooms, two baths, and a thirty-year mortgage. Owning a home was worth all the lean years of saving. Now they were free to decorate and furnish and just enjoy the knowledge that it was theirs, that their payments went to something substantial instead of to a landlord, and that if they wanted to change the trim or replace the doors or paint a giant peace sign on their roof, they could do so without explaining to anyone.

What they didn't own—and in San Francisco, it was possible to do just fine without one, so reliable was the public transportation—was a car. Not generally a problem, but on this particular

Friday evening, they'd gone to the supermarket. They needed everything, it seemed: food, cleaning supplies, utensils, toiletries. Over the past few weeks they'd been too busy to keep up on day-to-day items, and in the frenzy of packing their apartment to move, they had tossed many of their old things. So now they found themselves laden with plastic grocery bags, like pioneers crossing the continent carrying all their worldly goods.

"Maybe," Kevin found himself saying as the plastic straps bit into his wrists, "we should have found a place a little closer to the bus line."

Marianne smiled at him, struggling with three heavy bags of her own. "It won't always be like this," she assured him.

"No," he agreed with a dismayed chuckle. "Sometimes it'll be worse. Just wait until we need to bring home a few hundred pounds of sheep rock to finish the basement."

"We don't have a basement," she reminded him. "And it's Sheetrock, not sheep rock."

Kevin laughed. "I always wondered why it was called that."

"Anyway," she continued, "if it's really a problem, we could just buy a car."

Kevin had known she would say that—she had wanted one as long as they'd been together. He was adamant, though, that no one in San Francisco really needed a car. And if it wasn't necessary, why pay for insurance, and licenses, and parking? Why contribute to global warming and the hole in the ozone layer? There were just too many good reasons to not have a car, and only one good reason—well, four, if you counted aching arms and shoulders as separate reasons—to get one. "Let's not start on that," he warned her.

She laughed at his response. "It's only another block," she said cheerfully. The evening was warm for San Francisco, with just a hint of the usual crispness in the air, and Marianne glistened from the effort. Her long blond hair caught the glow from a streetlight and haloed her head, and the sight of that combined with the joyful peal of her laughter reminded him of how much in love he still was.

He was about to say something else, when he was distracted by a pair of headlights on the hill—except that he realized there was no hill there, that this was one of the flatter sections of San Francisco. Which meant those couldn't be headlights, even though that was what they looked like. A pair of bright lights, anyway, moving rapidly through the darkness, cutting a swath before them. "Marianne," he said, pointing, conscious of a quiver in his voice. "Look."

But he couldn't say any more, because the lights darted off to the left, and then charged right again, zigzagging like no airplane or helicopter could possibly do. They skimmed barely a dozen feet above rooftops, then shot out over the park, and when they zoomed back into sight, they were lower still. By now, Marianne was staring at the lights, too, both she and Kevin speechless with awe. Kevin was trying to gather his thoughts, to form a coherent sentence, when the lights suddenly rushed right over their heads. A blast of air accompanied them, as if a plane had flown right over, and Marianne let out a wordless scream. Instead of flying past, though, the—whatever it was, Kevin couldn't put a name to it—came to an abrupt halt behind them, then spun around and shot toward them again. Kevin's hands went limp; he felt the bags slipping from them, heard glass breaking on the sidewalk, but all as if from a great distance, like he was far away, observing himself from the other side of a semi-opaque window.

Get a grip, he mentally commanded. He blinked a couple of times, knowing that he was overreacting to something that must have had some kind of rational explanation. Kevin Haas was a rational guy, after all, a software engineer, the kind of man other people turned to when they wanted a level head to help solve a problem. He wasn't sure how he'd explain what had just happened—or *seemed* to have happened—but probably it had to do with working too much, with pushing himself too hard, coming home from the office every night to help out with everything that had to be done at the house. There were *no* lights in the sky, had probably never been anything but distant headlights reflecting off a cloud or something. He had over-reacted, and now he'd have to clean up a huge mess and probably go back to the supermarket later for whatever had broken.

Except when he looked at the sidewalk, there were no bags, no broken glass, no smashed eggs. His bags still hung from his arms, slicing into his wrists and fingers. And Marianne was—

—Marianne was nowhere. He turned this way and that, peering into the darkness. But the street was well lit, with houses pressing against it on both sides. He called her name, shouted it with every ounce of volume he could muster. Lights clicked on in house windows, people stepped out of their doors to see what the fuss was.

No Marianne. No bags on the ground, nothing to indicate that she was ever here with him.

As he scanned for her, he thought he glimpsed some strange lights, flickering once over Golden Gate Park, but then they were gone. A strange odor, like applesauce with cinnamon, lingered in the air.

And Kevin Haas was alone.

Chapter

1

The innocent's name was Barbara Hunsaker, and she was a new accounts manager at a bank in San Francisco's Financial District. She was also, at this moment, upside down. A Spinning Demon—a low-rent version of the powerful Spider Demon, with a similar MO, but nowhere near her power—had her trapped in his web, like a very large spider with an equally over-sized fly.

But the Halliwell sisters—well, two of the three, anyway—were on the case. Piper had been called away because of an emergency at P3, the nightclub she owned, and Phoebe and Paige were convinced that the Spinning Demon wouldn't be a problem for the two of them. They had shooed Piper off to deal with the plumbing crisis—P3, after all, being the household's major source of income, as well as a special source of

6

pride for Piper. They had tracked the Spinning Demon to its lair, in an abandoned warehouse near the Embarcadero. The place smelled like seafood after it's been left a few days in the sun, and Phoebe was starting to think she would rather burn her shoes than try to scrape off whatever blackish gunk she was stepping in. It'd be over in a few minutes, though. They'd vanquish the Spinning Demon, get Ms. Hunsaker safely back to her home, and all would be right in the world again.

At least, until the next demonic emergency.

That was why the world had the Charmed Ones. There would always be a next emergency, and a next one, and one after that. Innocent people would always need protecting from evil forces they didn't understand, couldn't even conceive of in their most horrible imaginings. Someone had to stand between the darkness and the light. That someone was the Halliwells. They bore the responsibility gladly, even when—as tonight—it meant giving up the chance to sit at home together, watching old movies on TV while they downed a half gallon of Choco-fudge Ripple.

With whipped cream, and cherries.

Remembering the ice cream made Phoebe furious all over again. "You might as well give it up," she told the Spinning Demon. "You know you don't have a chance against us."

The Spinning Demon backed away from them,

hands extended like claws, legs spread wide for balance. Its arms joined its torso at a spot that would have been midway down the ribs if it had been human. The demon's purplish black flesh was ridged all over. In the darkness of the warehouse, Phoebe couldn't get a better look at it. *Which is fine,* she thought, *because what I can see looks pretty hideous.*

It spat something at them—*should have been called a Spitting Demon, I guess*—which hit the floor and sizzled. *Acid. Got to make a point of avoiding that.*

Without speaking, she and Paige stepped away from each other, making themselves more difficult targets.

They continued to advance slowly, and it kept backing away, toward an open doorway that faced onto the water. The breeze that blew in was cold and sharp. From what Phoebe remembered, Spinning Demons couldn't swim, so she wasn't too worried about it escaping that way. From the rafters, a cocoon of webbing gave out muffled cries. *Barbara Hunsaker,* Phoebe realized. *We need to finish this up fast.*

"Let's take him!" she shouted. Using her powers of levitation, she floated in the air, and it reared up to follow her, temporarily losing its balance. Paige took advantage of the moment and hurled a vial at it—a vial that contained a vanquishing potion she'd whipped up earlier for precisely this purpose.

It hit the demon—except, it didn't exactly hit, but sailed right through the empty space where the demon had been a fraction of a second before, and splashed into the water behind it.

"Where'd it go?" Paige asked.

"I have no idea," Phoebe said. They both ran forward. There was no sign of him in the black waters outside, no telltale ripple.

The thing dropped toward them on a silken line.

"Geez, it's fast!" Paige shouted, ducking away from it.

Phoebe dodged it as well, shooting up into the air again as it came down. She fired a good, solid kick at it as they passed. She felt its solid, slightly furred flesh give under her boot, and the thing let out an unpleasant squeal.

When it hit the ground, the demon skittered around in a semicircle, moving with incredible speed. Paige had her arm cocked back to hurl another vial, but it loosed a stream of thick, sticky webbing that snared her arm, driving her backward where arm and vial alike were glued to one of the warehouse's walls.

"Phoebe!" Paige screamed.

Phoebe touched down lightly behind the demon, releasing two more quick kicks. The beast cried out again. Phoebe didn't mind touching it with her boots, but was hoping to not have to go hand to hand with such a disgusting creature. She would if she had to, of course—but what she really wanted was for Paige's vanquishing potion to do the trick.

When it spun around to attack Phoebe, she levitated again, shooting up over the demon. Its stream of webbing sailed into the air harmlessly. Phoebe landed beside Paige and she grabbed her sister's arm, helping tear it free from the Spinning Demon's gooey web.

"Never mind that!" Paige cried, orbing out of the worst of the webbing. "Here!" She shoved yet another vial into Phoebe's fist. "Just nail it!" Paige urged.

As Phoebe turned around to face it, the demon was letting loose another stream of its webbing. She took to the air, and once again the web stuff missed her, but hit Paige squarely across the middle, cementing her again to the wall.

Phoebe had the vial now, though. The demon again shot a strand straight up, intent on avoiding the vial by using the same stunt that it had the last time. But that time, Paige had been throwing across, so rising into the air had enabled it to avoid her throw. This time, Phoebe was above, hurling down. All that the demon accomplished by clambering quickly up its webbing was to increase the force with which the glass vial smashed against its back. The Spinning Demon flared with a bright orange light, screeched painfully, and was gone.

"Good shot!" Paige called. She had freed

herself from the wall again, but the webbing was all over her. "Now get this stuff off of me!"

Phoebe dropped to the ground, ready to comply. They needed to get Barbara Hunsaker down, too, she knew. As soon as she touched the clingy webbing, which was halfway between a solid and a liquid, she knew it was going to be a long, unpleasant chore.

Phoebe loved working at the *Bay Mirror*. Except on those days when her editor, Elise, ran the newspaper like Genghis Khan might have, had the ancient Mongol hoped to rule the world the modern way, by controlling mass media, instead of through the old-fashioned method of conquest and pillage.

This was, sadly, one of those days. Elise was on a tear about something—Phoebe had tried to tune out the specifics. *I do my job the best I can,* she thought. Beyond that, she didn't care to get into the internal politics of it any more than was absolutely necessary. Instead, she kept her distance, hunkered down, and read about the problems of ordinary San Franciscans.

And not so ordinary ones, she thought, putting down a letter from a man who wanted advice on how to handle visits from his dog's mother-in-law. *The thing is, it doesn't sound like he's making this up. Which means that his dog actually has a mother-in-law*—who visits—*or at the very least, he* believes *it does.*

She wasn't sure which was worse, and she was equally stumped about how she could help him. *We'll come back to you, Paul in Potrero Hill.*

It was surprising how many letters still came via the post office instead of e-mail. Phoebe couldn't remember the last time she'd sat down with a pen and written an actual letter instead of just typing at the keyboard and clicking "Send." Maybe there was something soothing in putting one's problems down on paper, folding them up, and sending them away in a sealed envelope. There were spells that worked in similar fashion. One would write a problem down on paper, say a few appropriate words, and bury or burn the paper. *I guess these are ritualistic cries for help,* she thought, looking at the bundles of mail stacked on her desk.

She preferred regular mail for this job, anyway, because with e-mail there was no physical connection to the letter-writer. Sometimes just touching the letter itself gave her a sense of the person who had written it, or she got a vibe from it that allowed her to phrase her answer in the most helpful way.

As soon as Phoebe touched the next letter in the stack, she knew that the person who had written it had a genuine problem. She felt a flash of fear, bordering on panic. *Someone should be calling 911 instead of writing to an advice columnist,* she thought, making a mental note of the Noe Valley return address.

Taking a quick look around to make sure she wouldn't be disturbed, Phoebe opened the letter. It started off the normal way: "Dear Phoebe. I love your column and read it all the time." People seemed to think they needed to butter her up to get her attention.

After the pleasantries, though, this letter quickly took a turn for the strange. "I'm afraid that my sister has been taken by space aliens. She isn't the same since they brought her back, and I think maybe they did something to her. But she can't remember what, and won't talk to me about them. All she wants to do now is exercise, and I'm afraid it's going to make her sick. How can I help her and get back the sister I used to know?"

Phoebe's natural reaction would have been to wad this one up and throw it in the trash, suspecting it was just some prankster out to make her look bad by responding to patently absurd mail. But the sensations she got from this one, the sense of impending doom, the indistinct flashes of beings that felt threatening, even though she could make out no detail . . . these things made her think twice about tossing it.

The letter was signed by Kara Bodine. The signature had a youthful flourish to it—Phoebe wouldn't have been surprised if the "i" in Bodine had been dotted with a heart, or perhaps a flower. But it wasn't. If Kara Bodine was, in fact, normally the kind of person who would do such a thing, whatever was troubling her had squelched that impulse.

And there was one other factor that stopped Phoebe short. She pushed back from her desk, folded the letter, and stood up. Bill Conason was a reporter on the Metro beat, and while she didn't know him that well, she'd had conversations with him from time to time. Recently, she'd overheard him talking by the watercooler, and she thought perhaps he'd have some insight into this situation.

Phoebe's spike-heeled, ankle-wrap sandals clicked as she crossed the newsroom toward Bill's desk, and she knew when he looked up at the approaching sound that he'd cast an admiring glance at her strappy, scoop-cut olive top and low-rise camouflage-pattern pants. That was okay with her—he was the kind of guy who'd look and enjoy without making a pretense at hiding his enjoyment. At the same time, she knew he wouldn't hit on her, and that once he'd had his glance he'd talk to her face, not to other bodily parts, and he'd respect her for her mind and not her body.

Men like him were actually a rarity in the news business, she was beginning to believe. Maybe in the rest of life too. She liked him and, most importantly, she thought he'd take this seriously even though she couldn't explain to him why she did, too, without revealing that she was a witch, and she had no intention of doing that.

Her prediction turned out to be right on the money. He heard her coming, glanced away from his computer, looked her up and down once, and then fixed a sincere smile on his face. "What's up, Phoebe?"

She wheeled a chair over from an empty desk—most of the Metro reporters were out covering the SoMa story, the discovery of more than a dozen dead bodies being a major news event—and rolled up close to him, so she could speak in low tones. Phoebe had already determined that the body discovery—while horrific in its own right—was human-on-human violence, and nothing the Charmed Ones should be looking into. "Did I hear you right the other day?" she asked. "Saying something about reports of UFOs over the city?"

He hesitated before answering, as if weighing his words carefully. "You did," he said after a few moments. "Why?"

Phoebe wagged the letter at him without handing it over. "This letter is from someone who claims her sister was abducted," she explained. "I just wanted to know if maybe there had been a rash of similar stories lately, along with the sightings."

Bill allowed himself a sardonic smile. "You must get letters like that all the time, Phoebe." He waved a hand around as if to encompass the whole city. "This is San Francisco, after all. World capital for crazies and freaks, right?"

"Maybe so," she admitted. "But I try to give everyone the benefit of the doubt. At least until they've proven somehow that they don't deserve it."

"That's very noble of you, Phoebe," Bill said. "And the kind of attitude that would kill a reporter from exhaustion before he could even begin to write."

Phoebe tossed him a grin. "Good thing I'm a columnist instead of a reporter."

"I'll say," he agreed. "So, you were asking about the UFOs."

"Uh-huh," Phoebe said, encouraging him with a nod.

"Yes, there have been lots of reported sightings. Even more than usual. Lights in the sky; saucer-shaped objects at dusk; airplanes that fly too low, dart around oddly—the usual kind of thing, just more of it. And from some fairly solid citizens too—you know: cops, mail carriers, firefighters. A pilot or two. The kind of people you can't just write off."

"But I haven't seen anything about it show up in the paper," Phoebe observed.

"I said you can't write them off," Bill reminded her. "That doesn't mean they can substantiate what they said. In a city like this, a forty-percent increase in UFO sightings still isn't news. Not unless there's something to back it up. Photos, video, a hundred people all seeing the same thing at the same time. So far, none of that has happened. So it's just rumor, not news—here, anyway. If you'd read the tabloids you'd see that they're playing it up for all it's worth."

Phoebe shrugged. "Guess I'm reading the wrong papers."

"So I don't know what to tell you about your letter," Bill said. "Personally, I think it's just another trend, like overpriced coffee and designer cell phones. But I guess both of those are here to stay, so what do I know?"

"Thanks, Bill," she said. "Let me know if it goes from rumor to news, okay? Or if people start building mountains in their mashed potatoes."

He raised a thumb toward the ceiling. "Deal," he assured her. "And if you hear about anyone hiding ETs in with their stuffed animals, you let me know." He turned back to his computer screen before she left, but as she walked away, she was convinced that his gaze didn't stay there until after she was out of sight.

Chapter
2

"Flying saucers?" Piper said, incredulous. "Aliens with big eyes, and fingers that glow in the dark? Or maybe the kind with fishbowl helmets and ray guns?"

"Be nice," her husband admonished her. They were in the Halliwell living room, Leo and Piper sitting together on the couch, Paige sprawled on one chair, and Phoebe on the floor with her back to the wall. Phoebe had brought the letter home from the paper, but she had waited until after dinner to bring it up. "Obviously Phoebe doesn't think it's quite so ridiculous."

Piper looked to her youngest sister for support. "What about you, Paige? I'm surprised you haven't said anything. You're normally all over this kind of silliness."

Paige looked at the floor, Piper noted, instead of at any of them, and her peaches-and-cream complexion turned rosy. "Maybe I'm not so sure it's silly," she said hesitantly.

"Oh, spare me," Piper said. She and her sisters were witches, and they'd seen a lot of strange things in their time—demons, wood nymphs, leprechauns, and more. *But Martians? Little green men from space?* Some things were just too far out there, even for her. "Even if there were aliens—and that's a really huge *if*—why would they abduct someone in order to make her want to exercise? What's the point of that?"

"It's not just the letter, Piper," Phoebe reminded her. "It's the vibe I got from it. Like a vision, almost. Only not."

"Well, that's convincing," Piper said sarcastically.

"But the thing is, I don't know which sister I'm getting it from," Phoebe told them. "If it's a vibration from the abducted sister instead of the one who wrote the letter, then it's not surprising that it's muted and vague."

"She makes a good point," Leo said. He was bending over backward to remain neutral, which Piper found strangely annoying.

"What if there are visitors from another planet?" Paige brought up. "After all, there have been reports, and sightings, almost as long as there's been recorded history. The number of planets out there is practically infinite. Who says we're the only one with intelligent life on it?"

"Right now I'd settle for a room with intelligent life in it," Piper grumbled.

"I had a professor back at Berkeley," Paige went on, "who made exactly these points. We have no idea what's on the planets outside our own solar system. We're mostly just guessing on the ones inside it. There are millions and millions of planets that might possibly support life, and nothing to say that some of those civilizations couldn't have developed space travel."

"Was that his lesson plan?" Piper sniped, feeling betrayed by the sister she had expected to back her up on this. "Or his screenplay?"

"Piper, if you're not even going to admit to the slight possibility that this is on the level, then I'm sorry I brought it up," Phoebe said. She spoke with such apparent melancholy that Piper was sorry for having blasted her so hard. But the whole thing was just so . . . so *stupid*!

"I'm sorry too," Piper said, knowing that there was way more on her mind these days than just Phoebe's alien-abduction problem. "I've seen plenty of things that most people would think were impossible or inexplicable. I should try to be more understanding."

"It's just . . . I can't help feeling that maybe there's really someone in trouble here," Phoebe continued. "Not the kind of trouble that I can fix with a snappy reply in my column, but the kind that calls for the Charmed Ones."

"I'll tell you what," Piper offered, hoping to bring the conversation to a quick end. "If you find out that there's more to this than just the paranoia of a crazy person, we can look into it."

Phoebe beamed, and seeing her happiness, Piper was again a little ashamed of taking such a hard-line stance. But only a little. "Deal," Phoebe said. "I'll check it out tomorrow."

"And I'll try to track down that professor," Paige suggested. "I think his name was Hayman, Haywood, something like that."

"Would you, Paige?" Phoebe asked. "I'd appreciate that."

"Knock yourselves out," Piper said, stretching and standing up. "It's not like we have anything more important to deal with."

She left the room and found a quiet spot in the conservatory to sit and think. But she'd only been there a few moments when Leo came in and sat down beside her, a frown of concern furrowing his forehead. "Something bothering you, sweetheart?" he asked.

Piper fixed him with a glare that she hoped spoke volumes. "You mean besides the fact that my husband won't take my side when my sister comes up with such an obviously ridiculous statement?" she asked sarcastically.

He sat across from her, his hazel eyes blinking in surprise. "Why is it so ridiculous?" he asked. "I mean, sure, it sounds a little wacky. But we've encountered some wacky things. We know there are several planes of existence, so why not existence on other planets, too?"

Piper pointed at him. "That's it exactly," she declared. "If there are aliens among us, don't you think the Elders would be up on it? And wouldn't they have said something?"

Leo pursed his lips, considering for a moment before answering. "Seems reasonable."

A sudden and horrible thought occurred to Piper. "If you had been told about something like that, you'd share—right? You wouldn't hold out on your wife and your sisters-in-law."

"Of course not," Leo objected. "I mean, of course I wouldn't hold out on you. There's been no talk of aliens that I've heard about. Just the usual suspects. That doesn't necessarily mean anything, though—there's plenty they don't tell me unless I have a particular reason to know."

"Well, aliens in San Francisco, abducting people and making them"—Piper could barely get through this part without a laugh—"making them exercise? Surely that's something they'd alert you to."

"Seems like," Leo relented. "On the other hand, even if Phoebe's way off base on this, it also seems like you'd normally cut her a little more slack. That's why I'm wondering if there isn't more going on."

It was Piper's turn to hesitate, not sure of how much of what was on her mind she wanted to talk about. *And he's right about that*, she thought,

it's not just Phoebe's silly letter that's bugging me.
She decided to take it a step at a time, reveal the
outer problems but hold back the deeper ones
until she was certain she wanted to reveal them.
Piper had always been a firm believer in solv-
ing her own problems whenever possible, in
keeping her own house in order without help
from anyone.

Even someone she loved as much as Leo.

She looked at him, sitting across from her, clad
in a dark blue, long-sleeved T-shirt and white
jeans, looking at her expectantly with a patient,
hopeful expression. As much as Piper believed in
taking care of things herself, Leo believed in fixing things for people. He hated to leave someone
with a problem if there was a chance he could do
something to help. He could probably help now,
but there were two problems with that. One,
instead of accepting help, she wanted to learn to
cope with the situation herself so she wouldn't
feel defeated by it. And two, when it came to the
deeper issue, Leo was part of the problem. To
enlist his aid, she'd have to tell him about it.

"It's P3," she said finally, determined to skate
across the surface of things. "Specifically, the
plumbing."

"The plumbing?" he echoed.

"That's right. The plumbing crisis. It's gotten
worse. A bad thing, at a nightclub. Pipes backing
up, ooky, not to mention on the stinky side. So I
hired a plumber to come and fix it."

"You could have called me," Leo said. *True to form.*

"Leo, it's a business, and I made a business decision. I hired a professional. At least, I thought he was at first. He looked professional, you know, tool belt and loose pants. Most of the time he was working on pipes, I was looking the other way and might have missed some of what he was saying. Anyway, he just made things worse. Ditto plumber number two. They came in, they talked the talk, they worked the wrenches, and they did absolutely nothing to fix the problem."

Piper drew in a deep breath, blew it out, and continued. She knew Leo's handyman background would kick in. He obviously trusted her to run things at the club, and he had plenty on his plate, like helping track down the Spinning Demon that Phoebe and Paige had vanquished earlier. But he still had that gut reaction to Piper spending money on stuff that he knew how to do. "So now we get to plumber number three. Same story. The company has a good rep—this time, I checked. A woman this time, and she can do the job, but it's going to cost four thousand dollars to fix it."

Leo whistled. "Four grand for a plumbing problem?"

"If I'm lucky," Piper added. "If we don't have to tear up the street in front of the club. Because then it'll be *expensive.* That's her word. Like four thousand bucks is some kind of bargain."

"Wow."

"Right, wow. So now I guess I'm having a crisis of confidence. Because maybe these first two plumbers I hired just made a small problem worse. Or maybe this woman is trying to rip me off. Normally I have no problem handling this kind of thing. I'd have told this woman to just go ahead and bring in her crew, get the work done. But now I'm just not sure. Do I bring in yet another plumber to offer a fourth opinion? And maybe make things worse? I just don't know."

Leo nodded his head sagely. "I could still take a look at it."

"You're a good handyman, Leo," Piper said. "And a great Whitelighter, but I don't think either of those talents will fix this problem. Plus, I'm sure you've got more important things to deal with. And besides . . ." She offered a smile as she said this, and was gratified when he returned it. "I'm not sure I want you coming home from the club as stinky as these other plumbers were after they rooted around in the pipes for a while."

He seemed to understand her hesitation. That was one good thing, among many, about Leo—he picked up on even subtle cues. Not everybody did, she knew. "I'm sure you'll make the right call," he told her. "If you want me to come in, even just to talk with the plumbers, I'd be happy to. If you want to handle it yourself, that's okay too."

"Thanks, Leo," she said. "I appreciate the offer."

He stifled a yawn. "No problem," he said. "That's what I'm here for. But not right now. Now I'm going to bed."

"I'll be up in a few," Piper assured him.

"Okay." He rose and walked toward the stairs, leaving her alone in the conservatory.

What she had told her husband was the truth, about the plumbers and how they had shaken her confidence in her ability to do her job right. But there was more to it than that, she knew. She was upset that, the night before, her sisters had so readily agreed that they could handle the Spinning Demon without her. Sure, she'd had the problem at the club. And if she hadn't attended to it then, it might have developed into something even worse, though she couldn't see how, at this moment, it could be worse. But even though she'd been wrong—even though they really didn't, it seemed, need her—they hadn't even thought that they did. She might as well have been an adjunct Charmed One, a reservist to be called up only when absolutely necessary. She didn't like that feeling at all. Nor did she care for the inescapable sensation that her life was consumed by two things: being a Charmed One (adjunct or no), and work. This whole plumbing business had just reinforced to her how tied down she was by the club, leaving her no time to make new friends, develop new hobbies, travel, or do much of anything else. It seemed lately like every waking moment was given over to one chore or the other, while life's pleasures happened without her.

And to make things even worse, she'd been downtown with Leo the day before, and had caught him checking out a couple of nubile young cuties window-shopping outside a lingerie store. She didn't really mind that—everyone looked sometimes, herself included. But he denied it when she commented, and it was that, more than the looking, that troubled her. Why would he lie about something so basic?

The only reason she could come up with was that the look hadn't been as innocent as she had believed, at first. That maybe he wasn't interested in just looking, but in taking some sort of action, as well. The two of them had been talking about trying to have a baby, and maybe in his mind she had already gone from young wife and companion to mother, middle-aged and stodgy. He still told her that he loved her, that he found her beautiful and desirable. But was she? Had she somehow slipped from sexy to maternal without noticing?

That's it, she told herself. *You're reading way too much into this. Just go to bed.*

After all, tomorrow you have to deal with stinky pipes.

Chapter
3

But sleep wasn't going to come easily for Piper that night, she knew. With the rest of the household snoozing away, she found herself back in the living room, hoping that something on late-night TV would take her mind off her own problems long enough to let her crash. She sat on the couch across from the TV, mindlessly punching the CHANNEL UP button. Old bad movie, twenty-four-hour news, newer bad movie, inane talk show, cartoons—that held her interest for a moment, until she realized it was a cartoon from her childhood that she particularly hated. She pushed MUTE so she wouldn't have to hear the voices. Channel up, channel up.

Finally, a face came on the screen that caught her eye, a face that looked familiar at first glance, though she didn't immediately know why. It was a woman's face, pretty but not beautiful, and with no makeup whatsoever. Platinum blond hair was held off the face with a terry headband. The woman's eyes were clear and blue, as blue as deep mountain lakes, and a glimmer of intelligence shone in them. She was talking, her mouth open to reveal straight, even white teeth. Her jaw was firm. A no-nonsense woman, Piper thought, someone with strong ideas and the self-confidence to carry them out. She wasn't sure why she read so much into just a face, but she did, and it made her want to see more.

Then the camera zoomed out. The woman was wearing a tight pink leotard, gray cotton gym shorts with a pink stripe, and sneakers. Her body was great—hard where it should be, supple and lithe, curved in the right spots. The camera kept moving back, and Piper could see that she was in a gym setting, with a couple dozen women around her, sitting on mats, watching her. They were wearing workout clothes, too, and perspiration stains on their backs revealed that they had been exercising. Now, though, the woman at the front of the group was just talking. Piper turned the sound up to an audible level.

". . . back your own bodies, and take back your own lives," she was saying. "No one but you has the right to dictate what your shape should be. Some of you are going to be thin, some of you are going to be muscular, some of you are going to be rounder, or taller, or perkier, than those around you. That's just life. That's just the variety of human existence. That's what makes things interesting. The important thing is, you have the body that you are supposed to have. Exercise can firm and tone you, but it won't make a short woman tall. And it shouldn't.

"The ideal you still contains the word 'you.' You are not your sister, your neighbor, your best friend, or a model on a magazine cover. You are you, and no one else. So the ideal you is simply the best *you* you can be, and the Meg Winship Ideal You program can help you achieve that. If being your best you, the ideal you, sounds good to you, then keep watching. If you want to become someone else, change the channel now. We're going to be working on being us."

Piper left the channel on, mesmerized by this woman and her simple, upbeat message. The woman, who Piper now understood was Meg Winship, author of some very popular fitness books, led the group on-screen through a series of exercises that looked fun as well as challenging.

Before she quite realized it, Piper was on the floor in her loose cotton pajamas, joining in.

Phoebe Halliwell's face was all over the city—on buses, billboards, and newspaper boxes, from the Wharf to the Mission, from Bay Bridge to Golden Gate Park. Sometimes that was a huge ego boost. Others, it was just plain annoying.

Today was one of the latter, since she had

intentionally gone into a newsstand where no one knew her, only to see her face plastered on a poster provided by the *Bay Mirror*. She could only hope the proprietor, and the few customers in the place, didn't pay it any attention. Knowing her mission, she had worn a simple outfit of blue jeans, and a snug yellow crop top with a big red 2 emblazoned on the front. With an Oakland A's ball cap and sunglasses on, she figured she was as incognito as she could get. Plus, the day was bright and sunny and warm—all unusual for San Francisco—so the cap and shades had the added benefit of practicality.

She had come for the city's tabloids, and this place seemed to have them all. They had names like *Weekly Scoop*, the *SF Tattler*, and the *InSider*. Phoebe normally steered clear of such absurdities, not understanding how anyone could be taken in by their breathless tales of Elvis sightings, three-hundred-pound babies, vampire cats, and, yes, space aliens. Even worse, though, she thought, was the celebrity gossip—*like people who act in a movie aren't entitled to a private life anymore*. She didn't need to know who was sleeping with whom, who'd had liposuction or a face-lift, who was on the outs with her mother or her daughter or her ex-best friend and manager.

Doing her best to be inconspicuous, Phoebe bought them all, half a dozen tabloids with screaming headlines and ridiculous photos. She took them to a quiet coffee shop decorated with

hundred-year-old photos of San Francisco—
pre-earthquake—ordered an iced low-fat white-
chocolate mocha, and read through them.

Bill Conason was right. The UFO story may
have been roundly ignored by the mainstream
press, but the tabloids had run with it, complete
with blatantly doctored photos. San Francisco's
famed Alamo Square in a shot of Victorian
houses she had seen a thousand times, except
with something resembling a pie tin amateur-
ishly pasted into the sky. A gray-skinned alien
she was pretty sure she'd seen in a movie stood
between the mayor and the police chief in a
photo that she believed had come from the *Bay
Mirror*, except that in the original, a U.S. senator
had been standing where the alien was now.

As nonsensical as the pictures were, though,
the stories were surprisingly consistent. People
reported seeing lights in the sky. Sometimes, the
lights came alarmingly close. On some occa-
sions, people had disappeared, though they had
all turned up later, unharmed. If it was some
kind of mass psychosis, it seemed to be a common one, and seemingly not dangerous.

With the exception of the UFO stories, most of
the tabloids had little in common with one
another. Some specialized in celebrity "news,"
one in stories of the supernatural—Phoebe paged
through this one with special interest, relieved to
see that none of the Charmed Ones' exploits
seemed to have been witnessed or reported—

some in pseudo-political muckraking, accusing local politicians of crimes and rip-offs great and small. There were a few features common to all: horoscope columns, opinion columns, household tips. There were even, she noted, some advertisers who bought space in all the tabloids, including a discount jewelry chain, a company that sold collectible plates featuring pictures of dead celebrities and religious figures, and a fitness guru advertising an upcoming rally.

As she closed the last of the papers, Phoebe didn't feel especially enlightened. She had known that she'd have to go see the woman who wrote her the letter, so that she could check out the sister. But before she did that she wanted to be armed with as much information as possible, to know if this was simply an isolated case, or one of many. And there did genuinely seem to be some kind of UFO fever gripping the city. But since she didn't ordinarily pay attention to these tabloids, she couldn't tell if that was unusual, or just another day in San Franscisco.

She just hoped Paige was finding out something a little more definitive.

"Paige Matthews, of course I remember you!"

He didn't, of course. Paige had found Dr. Carter Haywood, her old professor from the University of California at Berkeley, living in a run-down Craftsman house, all dark brown wood with a lightly slanted, shingled roof, in

Cow Hollow. He had answered the door with a broom in his hand and an apron tied around his middle, as though on a cleaning spree, and she'd had to identify herself three times, complete with the year she'd been in his class, before he claimed to know her. Then again, he had made an impression on her, but she hadn't exactly been the ideal student, much less teacher's pet. So of all the hundreds, maybe thousands, of students he'd taught over the years, there was no special reason why he should recall Paige.

"I was wondering if I could ask you a couple of questions, Dr. Haywood," Paige said tentatively. He was smiling, but he still brandished the broom, and she was half-afraid he'd try to sweep her off the front porch. She only remembered bits and pieces of his UFO theories—he had been a philosophy professor, and talking about UFOs, even in the face of administrative warnings, had eventually gotten him fired—and wasn't sure that he'd be receptive to questions about them.

"Of course, of course," he said, smiling broadly. He hadn't been a young man even when Paige was taking a class from him, but in the few years since then, he seemed to have aged a great deal. His face was creased, with heavy bags under his eyes, and jowls that drooped like a basset hound's. Thick glasses over his eyes made them seem to bulge out from his skull. His hair was gray and wispy, though he unconsciously patted it down as he stood back to invite Paige inside. He wore a gray cardigan sweater over his stooped form, with a buttoned-up blue shirt underneath it, shapeless gray pants, and black shoes. "Come in, please."

Seeing him here brought a flood of memories rushing back from her college days. His class had been in one of the campus's giant lecture halls. Paige invariably had been late, or close to it, dashing across the plaza toward class after everyone else had already taken their seats. A young man would play his guitar on the plaza most mornings, his case open for donations, and sometimes Paige would toss a quarter or two into the case as she scurried past.

Inside the lecture hall, the students had sat in auditorium-style seats while Dr. Haywood stalked the stage. He'd never seemed to need a single note, but had filled the class session with a monologue that began the moment the clock ticked nine, and didn't end until the hour was done.

Normally, his lectures were on appropriate subjects. He was a particular fan of Spinoza, she remembered, and Martin Heidegger. But Paige recalled one day when he'd gotten off on a tangent about the difference between actual and perceived reality, and he'd somehow found himself talking about alien visitors. "There could be some among us right here," he had insisted, "right in this room. Take a look at the classmate to your right, to your left. Looks human, yes? But then ask yourself: If they had the technology to reach our planet, when we're still so hopelessly bound within our own solar system, wouldn't they also know enough to be able to project whatever reality we would expect to see? Surely they wouldn't take the trouble to come here and walk among us while keeping their own native form.

"What you see is not always what you get. And what you think you perceive is not always what's there."

He had shoved himself back on topic then, but students in the class had talked for weeks about his apparent belief in alien visitation. From what Paige had heard, in the year after that, his lectures had become more and more bizarre, until finally he was forced from his job.

When she entered the house, Paige wondered what he could have been cleaning. The home's architecture was beautiful, but virtually every horizontal surface seemed to be covered by books or papers. Manila file folders were everywhere—some thick as phone books, others holding just a page or two. Books towered in stacks on the floor, on chairs, and on the two tables that she could see from the entryway. There was hardly enough visible floor to sweep. A stale, dusty odor tickled Paige's nose, and she had to hold back a sneeze.

"Place is a little bit of a mess, I'm afraid," he said.

"That's okay. Did you live here when you were teaching at Berkeley?"

He chuckled, leading her on a circuitous route through the maze. "I don't miss that commute, I can tell you that. Before BART, it was almost impossible. But even after that, it was a pain."

Paige had taken the Bay Area Rapid Transit trains through the tunnel that ran under the bay, connecting San Francisco with the East Bay, enough times to know what he meant. It was much faster than driving the Bay Bridge, but at rush hour it got crowded and unpleasant. "I'm sure it was," she said. "It's a long trip, twice a day."

"But I couldn't give up this house," he went on. "And now I'm glad I didn't. I never go across the bay anymore. Hardly ever, anyway. Come in here, Paige, please."

He led her into a dining room with a huge, formal dining table in its center. Like the rest of the house, this room looked like someone had held a library over the roof and shaken all the books out. But at least there were chairs around the table. "Have a seat," he offered, and scraped another away from the table for himself.

In deference to the hot day, she'd worn a white floral print sundress, and now she feared that if the grime caking the rest of the house was also on the chairs, she'd wind up with a huge smudge on her bottom. But she sat, nose still tickling from all the dust. Maybe he'd kicked up more of it by sweeping, though she still couldn't see anyplace he might have been doing so. He had set the broom down someplace, but the apron was still cinched around his middle. "What I wanted to ask you about, Dr. Haywood," she began, figuring the best way to do this was just to dive right in, "was UFOs."

His face tightened at the sound of the word. "I . . . I don't know what you mean," he stammered.

"Come on, Dr. Haywood. Unidentified flying objects. You used to talk about them all the time in class."

"That's a bit of an exaggeration," he insisted. "I may have mentioned them once or twice, I suppose. Much to my later chagrin."

"Because you got fired?"

"I was a tenured professor. Untouchable, or so I thought. And teaching at a university with a well-known respect for diverse viewpoints. But somebody took exception to my occasional mention of an important, little known scientific phenomenon, and I was railroaded. And that, young lady, is all I really care to say on that subject."

His face had turned red, edging toward eggplant, and he tugged at the collar of his shirt as if it had suddenly become too tight. Paige had a mental image of him suffering a heart attack because she had come in here and badgered him about a sensitive topic. "If you really don't want to talk about it—"

"That is exactly what I want, Ms. Matthews, he snapped. "Not to talk about it. If you don't mind, I'm a very busy man."

"Please, Dr. Haywood," she replied urgently. She was afraid it was all slipping away because she had been too impatient to take her time getting around to the subject at hand. *It isn't*, she reminded herself, *necessarily all that important— just a matter of finding out if Phoebe's letter-writer is a lunatic or not.* There was no need to panic, but just the same, she didn't want to leave empty handed after taking the trouble to locate and visit the professor. "What I was going to say was, if you didn't really want to talk about it, you wouldn't have put your job on the line the way you did. That was an act of courage, Dr. Haywood. Now, there's nothing anyone can do to punish you further, so you've got to show the same courage. It's important."

"I don't see how it could be, young lady," he said. "Since it's nothing but a lot of balderdash."

"You didn't always think that."

"Sometimes young people are foolish. Sometimes old people are too. That doesn't mean we can't finally develop some intelligence."

Paige felt her mind spinning, trying to come up with an angle that would encourage Dr. Haywood to talk about his theories. From what little she remembered—she had taken the class,

after all, to learn about philosophy, not UFOs—
he had been convinced that Earth was visited
frequently, and he'd claimed to have evidence.
That, she believed, was what had finally got him
fired. Not the theory, but the plainly delusional
insistence that he could *prove* it.

Maybe it wasn't so delusional, though. Maybe
Phoebe's correspondent—well, her correspondent's sister, anyway—really had experienced
what she believed she had.

"I'm afraid I really must ask you to go now.
It's been lovely seeing you, but as I said, I'm terribly busy, and—"

"Wait, Dr. Haywood," Paige interrupted. The
way to pry it from him had just come to her. It
was risky. But she figured everyone already
thought he was just a crazy old man, so no one
would believe him if he reported what he was
about to see. "I just want you to know that there
really is an important reason for me to hear your
theories of UFOs."

"I have no theories—," he began.

Paige cut him off again. She focused on a particular red book, at the top of a stack on the far
end of the table. "Book," she said, holding her
hand out. The book orbed from its place on the
stack, showing up in her hand a moment later. A
simple trick, for her. She held it out toward Dr.
Haywood, and then placed it on the table before
him. "You want to see it again?"

"No, no." The expression on his face was one of

awe, but with something else mixed in. She wasn't sure, but she thought that maybe the other emotion was fear. "No, that's . . . that's remarkable."

She shrugged. "Not really. Pretty much an everyday thing for . . . for us." She left unsaid the part about how she was a witch. He would believe what he wanted to believe, and she didn't want to steer him in any other direction.

"Of course," he said, anxiety tightening his lips and cheeks. "But for mundane Earth people, it's . . . it's like a miracle."

Another shrug. "I suppose."

"Of course, it is," Dr. Haywood continued, the words tumbling from him in excitement. "Obviously the kind of matter-teleportation technology required for something like that— and nanoscopic, I would imagine, or else built into you in some way—is far beyond our capabilities. I'm sure it's beyond anything our scientists are even thinking about. That technology alone would have enormous consequences, world-changing ones. The global economy—if you took shipping and travel costs out of it, you'd have an entirely different economic picture. And the military applications would be enormous as well. Security considerations, antiterrorist measures—everything would have to be rethought. Simply amazing."

"Then you understand why I'm interested to know what your theories are," Paige suggested. "In detail, if possible."

"Yes, indeed. I do understand. But . . . well, this opens up a whole new realm of study for me, of course. I was busy, but now I have to discard so much, start over from ground zero. I'm afraid I really must get to work—"

"I'm busy, too, Dr. Haywood," Paige said, cutting him off before he went too far down that road. "If we could get to why I came."

Dr. Haywood nodded frantically, and Paige noticed that he had backed a few steps farther away from her. He seemed genuinely afraid of her now. "Yes, yes, of course. Just one moment." He rose from the table, went to a bookcase—he could use a few more of those, Paige thought—and withdrew a single volume from it. When he returned to the table, she recognized his name under the title: *The Visitors.*

"It's all in here," Dr. Haywood said. "Everything I've spoken about for years—I put it all down here. Take it. It will explain all of my theories to you, for right or wrong."

"Thank you," Paige said. This wasn't exactly what she'd been hoping for. She had wanted a quick summary of who the aliens might be and what they wanted here, not a homework assignment. *Once a teacher . . . ,* she thought.

"Again, I'm sorry to be so rude, but I really must ask you to go," Dr. Haywood said. "It's very nice to see you, but I've got so much to do."

"I understand," Paige said. She felt a little ashamed of herself for having tricked him, and for carrying on the charade now. But it had definitely opened the floodgates. She didn't think she had to worry he would spill the beans about her, at least. He seemed a little too spooked to say anything to anyone.

A few minutes later she was outside his house, book in hand. The day was just as sunny and warm as it had been, and three women in shorts and sports tops jogged past her, each wearing headphones. She couldn't tell if they were listening to music or what, but they had the oddest expressions on their faces—somewhere between self-satisfied and blissful. They glanced once at Paige, and then at Dr. Haywood's house, and then they sped up the block and were gone.

Chapter
4

The job of a police detective was a lot less glamorous than TV shows and crime novels made it appear. Today, for example, cops all over the city were investigating a series of multiple murders—possibly gang-related—south of Market, and here Darryl Morris was, chained to his desk.

But every detective was responsible for his or her own paperwork, and since Darryl's latest case had involved the Charmed Ones, the paperwork was more complicated than usual. Catching crooks was one thing, but cleaning up a case when the perpetrator had been vanquished by the Halliwell sisters was another matter entirely. From every indication, the murders being investigated were strictly human against human, and the Charmed Ones were not connected to it at all. Darryl was glad of that—otherwise, he'd have tried to dodge this paperwork a little longer so he could make sure they stayed out of the lime-light.

Paperwork was not, to put it mildly, Darryl's favorite part of the job. To stay alert through the miasma of forms, he drank so much bad police-station coffee that his stomach burned in protest. His back and neck were aching from the hours of sitting at his cramped desk.

So when a man walked into the office, with a worried expression on his face and a questioning look in his eyes, Darryl was thrilled at the prospect of a distraction. He rose, shaking off the kinks in his muscles. "Can I help you, sir?"

The guy turned to him, hollow-eyed, lower lip trembling. He was upset, that much was clear. "I . . . I hope so."

"Why don't you tell me about it?" Darryl asked. He should have offered the man a chair, but he didn't want to sit down himself yet. "I'm Detective Morris."

"My name is Haas, Kevin Haas," the man said. "My wife, Marianne . . . this is going to sound crazy, I know, completely insane, but I'm not insane. I'm an engineer, you know, I'm a steady, sensible guy."

"I'm sure you are," Darryl said soothingly. "Just tell me what happened, Mr. Haas."

"Well, we were walking home from the super-market, out in the Sunset district. And these lights came, like a . . . like a UFO, I guess. And they took Marianne. She was with me, and then after the lights flew away, she was gone."

"When was this?" Darryl asked him. Kevin Haas was right: It did sound insane.

"Last night," Kevin said.

"I see. And then what did you do?"

"Well, I . . . I looked for her. Tried calling her cell phone, you know, but she didn't answer. Finally, since I was only a couple of blocks from home, I went there to call the police. And there she was."

"She was at home?"

"Yes," Kevin replied. "She had gone shopping with me, but somehow the lights, the UFO, whatever it was, had picked her up and taken her home."

"What did she tell you about how she got there?"

"That's the thing. She didn't remember anything about it—didn't even remember having gone shopping with me. But I looked in the kitchen cabinets—all the groceries she'd been carrying had been put away, right where they belonged. So obviously I wasn't just nuts, she *had* been out with me, and she had been brought home, somehow."

"And you pointed this out to her?" Darryl asked. He wasn't as certain Haas wasn't a tad nuts.

"Yes, of course I did. But she didn't really want to talk about it. She was too busy exercising along with a videotape."

"Exercising?" Darryl echoed.

"That's right. Only the thing is, she never does those exercise tapes. She doesn't need to. We don't own a car, so she walks everywhere. To work and so on. But she doesn't do workouts like this. I don't even know where she got the tape. I think it was called *The Ideal You*, or something like that. Completely not her kind of thing. But she would barely look away from the TV or stop working out long enough to talk to me. She kept it up until long after I went to bed. Finally she came in and slept for a while, but when I got up this morning, she was at it again. I'm afraid she's going to, I don't know, hurt herself. Strain something, you know?"

"It's definitely an unusual situation, Mr. Haas," Darryl told him. "But I don't see that there's been a crime committed."

Kevin looked distraught at the idea that the police might not step in to help him. "What about kidnapping?"

"It sounds like she was released almost immediately," Darryl pointed out. "Not so much kidnapped as given a ride. If she is willing to come right out and say that she was forcibly assaulted, then we could start to build a case—although we'd have to know who to build it against."

"So you're saying you can't do anything?"

"I'm saying it's not clear what we can do," Darryl answered. "Your wife is back home. I

agree with you about the exercise thing—
pushing herself too strenuously on a new fitness
regime can be dangerous. But I think she needs
to see a doctor about that, not a cop."

"But there's . . . there's something out there,
Detective. Something grabbing people off the
streets and . . . and changing them. It's got to be
stopped."

"Tell you the truth, Mr. Haas, we've had a lot
of reports lately of unidentified flying objects in
the city. Much more than usual. Even some of our
own, SFPD officers, have reported seeing them.
Thing is, we haven't been able to verify them. It's
not like we can pull one over and give it a ticket,
check its driver's license and registration, right?"

"But . . . they're a public hazard."

"We don't know that, sir."

"Maybe you don't, Detective. But you haven't
seen Marianne!"

Darryl saw that the guy wasn't going to go
away easily. "Give me your address, Mr. Haas,
and I'll come by and check on you both in a day
or so, see how you're both doing."

Kevin Haas scowled and mumbled that he
wasn't crazy and should not just be dismissed,
as he wrote down his address on a piece of
paper Darryl provided. But since it was all he
was going to get, he took it and left without even
a thank-you. Of course, Darryl hadn't exactly
done much to be thanked for. It was true that
there had been quite a few UFO reports over the

last several weeks—enough of them that the brass had been giving some consideration to ways they might respond. But so far, no official course of action had been chosen. The plan seemed to be to take down the details of each report, and then ignore it.

Worked for Darryl. He had enough weirdness in his life, by virtue of knowing the Charmed Ones. The Halliwell sisters were powerful witches—good witches, who had helped him out many times—and he was the only cop on the force they trusted with their secret. Which meant that his life was plenty complicated as it was. Adding UFOs to it would only make things worse.

Still, he decided that he'd call the Halliwells later on, to see if they knew anything about the UFO situation. Seemed like it might be right up their alley.

A crew of four plumbers worked inside P3. They had two trucks parked outside, and various hoses and other items snaked inside and into the pipes. It was noisy and smelly, and Piper could only hope that all the effort—and all the money it was costing her—would fix whatever the problem was. She had decided to trust this crew, even if she knew it was based on nothing more than the same gut feeling that had led her to trust the earlier plumbers, the ones who had compounded her problem.

But there was no requirement that she stay

inside and watch them. Her supervision might mean that they would keep working instead of sitting around on her chairs, drinking her beverages. But she believed them to be professionals who were here to get the job done. And the noise, not to mention the stench, was really getting to her. She just hoped they'd be done early enough for her to give the place a thorough cleaning and airing out, or she wouldn't be able to open tonight.

Just to get away from the club—and the smell—for a while, she took a walk. Up a couple of blocks, then down two streets, and then back. *A little exercise,* she thought, *a little fresh air. Couldn't hurt.* At the corner where she had planned to turn right, she went left instead, almost as if she'd lost control of her own legs. But then she brightened, because she realized that by going left, she was passing a video store she would have missed otherwise.

But you don't need any videos, she told herself.

Nonetheless, she found herself inside the store a moment later, wandering past the racks of action flicks and romances, comedies and cartoons. The self-help section caught her eye, and there, prominently displayed, she saw the face of the woman she'd watched on TV the night before. *Meg Winship's The Ideal You.* She snatched the box off the shelf and carried it straight to the cashier.

Outside again, she meant to turn back toward

P3. But those plumbers would still be working for hours, she realized. There was time to go home and have a quick workout before she got back to them.

Plenty of time.

Kara Bodine came to the door when Phoebe knocked on it, and from the expression on her face, one might have thought that her visitor was a movie star, a president, or the pope.

"You're Phoebe, from the papers!" the woman exclaimed when she was able to operate her mouth.

"Hi, yes," Phoebe said, a little chagrined by the outpouring. She had taken off the cap and sunglasses, but she got the feeling this woman would have recognized her even with them on. "I'm Phoebe Halliwell."

"I . . . I wrote you a letter," Kara said. She was in her forties—older than Phoebe had expected, from the letter—with short, dark hair framing a plain face, and dark circles under her eyes. She didn't look like she'd had a lot of sleep lately. From somewhere deep in the house, loud music boomed.

"I know," Phoebe said. "I got it. That's why I'm here."

"That is so sweet!" Kara cried, bringing her hands up to her cheeks. "I can hardly believe you would do this!"

"To tell you the truth, it's not something I

usually do," Phoebe assured her. "But I thought I should, this time."

Kara again was momentarily speechless. "Would you like to come in?" she finally asked. "It's not much, but it's home."

"Sure," Phoebe said. "Thanks."

Kara led Phoebe inside, into a combination living and dining area. The music was much louder in here, and Phoebe winced a little.

"That's my sister, Daphne," Kara told her. "I talked about her, in the letter."

"That's right," Phoebe said. "I'm glad she's here, I was hoping to meet her too."

"Good luck tearing her away from Meg Winship," Kara said with a shrug.

"Meg who?"

"That music." Kara almost had to shout to be heard. "That's her Meg Winship video. I've been living with this for a week."

"Can I see her?" Phoebe asked. *I thought she was exaggerating in her letter when she said, "All she wants to do is exercise." But maybe not.*

"Sure," Kara said. She nodded toward a closed door and walked toward it. Phoebe followed. When Kara opened it, the music blasted through like a wave. Kara stepped to the side, obviously unwilling to go any farther. Phoebe went past her and into a family room, where all the furniture had been pushed up against a wall to make a big clear space in front of an entertainment center.

Daphne was on the floor, clad in pink workout clothes and doing stomach crunches in time to the beat of the music. She glanced and mouthed a word Phoebe couldn't hear. "Hi," Phoebe guessed.

"Hi, Daphne!" Phoebe shouted. "Do you think we could turn the volume down a little?"

"What?"

Phoebe crossed to the entertainment center and found the volume button on the TV. She pushed it and watched the on-screen display move from maximum down to a saner level. "Is this okay?"

Daphne looked past Phoebe toward the screen, as if afraid she might miss something important. She didn't stop exercising. "I guess."

"Your sister's a little worried about you," Phoebe told her. "She thinks maybe you're pushing yourself a little too hard with this exercise stuff."

"She should try it," Daphne said. "I feel great. I'm really getting empowered."

"That's great, Daphne. But, you know, there's something to be said for moderation, too."

Daphne shot her a frown. "Meg said that people would try to keep me from being the ideal me."

Phoebe shook her head. "No, that's not it at all," she said with a smile. "Be all you can be. It's just . . . you can't push yourself too hard, too fast. It's not good for you."

"No pain, no gain."

"But if you wind up in the hospital, then you'll lose all the progress you're making."

The woman leading the exercise on TV—Meg Winship, Phoebe supposed—switched from the stomach crunches to leg lifts. Daphne followed suit without responding to Phoebe's comment.

Phoebe decided it was time to change course. "Can I ask you about something else?"

Daphne smiled. Sweat rolled down her cheek. "Okay."

"Were you, um . . . abducted? Taken on some kind of spaceship?"

"Did my sister tell you that?"

"She mentioned it," Phoebe confirmed. "What can you tell me about it?"

Daphne did a few more leg lifts before answering. "Nothing," she said. "Kara says she saw the lights, and then I went away. I don't remember a thing."

Phoebe was struck by how nice Daphne seemed to be—obviously she didn't want anyone interfering with her workout, but beyond that she didn't seem to resent the questions. On the other hand, she didn't seem able to tell Phoebe much, either. It didn't really matter if she remembered or not—if she wouldn't tell Phoebe anything, there wasn't much point in pursuing the conversation. "Okay, thanks, Daphne," she said. She left the room, closing the door behind her. A moment later she heard the volume shoot back up to ear-shattering level.

Kara was sitting at the dining table when Phoebe came out. "See what I mean?" she asked.

Phoebe nodded. "She is definitely taking the workout thing beyond a healthy obsession," she said. "But as far as the UFO thing, she says she doesn't know anything about it."

"That's what she tells me too," Kara said. "I know it happened, though. It sounds nutty, I'm sure. But we were here, at home, and these lights shone in the window. When we went outside to look, Daphne was right beside me. But then she was gone, like they transported her onto the ship. Just like in *Star Trek* or something. I screamed, and the neighbors came out, but by then it had gone away. We were still outside—I guess I was hysterical—when we heard the music from inside. We went in and saw Daphne just where you did, exercising with that video."

"And that's not what she had been doing when you first saw the lights?"

"She never did that. We were eating ice cream and watching a Sandra Bullock movie. I didn't even know she had the tape."

"It had to come from somewhere," Phoebe suggested.

Kara nodded. "The question is, where? And how can I get her to stop?"

"Have you tried to just turn it off?" Phoebe asked. "Throw the tape away?"

Kara looked steadily at her. "I love my sister," she said. "And she loves me. But I think if I tried to do that, she'd kill me. I mean it. She gets mad when I just suggest she take a break. I really think she'd kill me."

Chapter
5

Meg Winship worked in longhand, writing her speech down with a ballpoint pen on a yellow legal pad. She put down a sentence, then scratched it out, thought a moment, and then wrote something slightly different, getting closer to her precise meaning. She knew there wouldn't be long to talk to her audience and she wanted to get her point across in exactly the right way.

She had made plenty of public appearances, in addition to writing three best-selling fitness books and releasing several videos. In every one of them, her message had been essentially the same. Women can empower themselves, she taught, by setting goals, taking control of their own bodies, and making themselves strong and fit, which would give them the self-confidence necessary to accomplish those goals.

No single talk she had given, though, no book

or video, had been as important as this one would be. Her audience would be huge, and this was her home turf. There would be no retreat if she was anything less than stellar. Every publication in the San Francisco Bay Area was running stories on her, and plastered with advertising for the rally. Book and video sales were booming, and the whole region was gripped with Winship fever.

The words she spoke had to be just right. Each word would carry two meanings: the literal one and the deeper, more important one. She couldn't afford to get tongue-tied. She paused, taking in the Marin County estate her gifts had already bought her, a chateau-style wonderland big enough to make her feel isolated sometimes, lonely behind its high walls.

Meg was as wealthy as she needed to be, with every material belonging she could possibly want. It wasn't money she was after this time. She had paid for the venue herself, and admission was free. No, this was about one of those increasingly rare things that money couldn't buy. This was about nothing less than power. And not the kind that came from writing a check to a politician. *That* power was cheap, by the standards she had in mind. This was much more dear.

That was what made it special. Meg smiled as she wrote down the next line. Another few days, and she would have everything.

• • •

Beaver Street led straight to Corona Heights Park. But "park" wasn't really the right word to describe this place. In a sea of homes and businesses, Corona Heights was a wild island. No one could build on the steep and rocky outcropping, so it was designated a park for mapmakers and city officials to explain why it was left undeveloped when so much expensive real estate surrounded it. In fact, hardly anyone climbed it; children avoided it, and it wasn't suited for jogging or other outdoors pursuits.

One thing it *was* good for was the ritual celebration of nature. Living in the middle of a big city, there were precious few spots the Halliwell sisters could go to commune with the world around them. The city's parks tended to be crowded, and they weren't about to advertise their special gifts. Corona Heights, then, offered an ideal spot—so ideal that, on the solstices, it was downright jammed with Wiccans. That had been three nights ago, though, which meant that tonight it would be quiet and untrammeled. No one went up there at night—there were no lights, for one thing, and the paths were hard to navigate even in daylight—so they would have the solitude and seclusion they wanted.

The hard part had been getting Piper to leave the TV behind. At first, Paige had thought it was kind of cute. Piper had put on sweatpants and a tank top and pushed the furniture away so she had room to duplicate the exercises she was watching on tape. Paige tried to talk to her, kid her a little about this sudden interest in fitness, but Piper had ignored her and kept on with her workout.

They were still there when Phoebe came home, Piper working out and Paige reading through the book Carter Haywood had given her.

Phoebe had positively blanched when she saw what Piper was doing, and watching. She had tried to eject the DVD from the player, and Piper had screamed at her. Paige couldn't remember ever seeing those two go at it like they had, and she'd witnessed some pretty hairy sister fights. After fifteen minutes of pointless shouting, Phoebe dragged Paige off to the kitchen.

"We've got to do something," Phoebe had insisted. "Where did she get that video?"

"I have no idea," Paige replied. "She was in there with it when I came home."

"It's part of this whole UFO thing," Phoebe complained. "I don't know how, or why, but it's all mixed up together." She told Paige about her visit with Kara and Daphne Bodine, and the Meg Winship tape the latter had been obsessed with. "She was acting just like Piper," she said. "Wouldn't stop exercising even to talk."

"I can see how that could be a bad thing," Paige said. "I mean, too much of anything is bad, even if it's good, right?"

"This has to be a strain on their hearts,"

Phoebe pointed out. "Not to mention the permanent muscle and tendon damage they could be doing. They've been enchanted or something. We have to come up with a counterspell, and fast."

They had been working on that when Paige remembered the date, and the Corona Heights ritual they had planned. If they performed a spell there to free Piper from whatever enchantment she was under, it would have an accelerated impact. And if it worked on her, maybe they could use it to help Daphne Bodine and anyone else who might have fallen victim to whatever dark magic was at work.

Piper had been unwilling to leave the TV, though. Phoebe unplugged it, while Paige restrained Piper so she wouldn't simply plug it back in. After another spirited argument—this time with Leo joining in—Piper had finally relented, agreeing to go to Corona Heights for the scheduled ritual. Paige orbed them, their white robes, and their accessories over, which was by far the easiest way to scale its cliffs at night. Leo didn't join them, instead returning to P3 to supervise continued plumbing work that, he said, was keeping the club closed for the night.

Piper groused a little during the early stages of the ritual, but she helped light the candles and set them at the five points of a pentangle scraped into the earth by previous celebrants, and she spoke the appropriate words along with her sisters. Paige felt a bit distracted herself up here. From the high cliffs at Corona Heights, one could see for vast distances across the city, and she kept catching herself looking for lights or swiftly moving shapes in the sky. She still didn't believe in UFOs, but all the stories she'd heard, combined with what she had read in Dr. Haywood's book, had left her on edge. Adding in the additional fact that Piper—whom she had always considered one of the most levelheaded people she'd ever met—had come under some kind of fitness-related trance only made things worse. Part of the point of coming out here was to reconnect with nature, but that only worked if one could open one's mind and heart to it, and Paige doubted she could put aside her worries for her sister, and her questions about the UFOs, long enough to do so.

Near the end of the ritual, the three sisters engaged in a call-and-response segment, where one would say a phrase and the other two would give the necessary answer. Except when it was Piper's turn, she missed her cue. Paige turned and saw her staring into the distance, face slack, eyes wide and unblinking. Piper had been holding an athame, but it had fallen from her hand and stuck, point down, in the earth. Her legs seemed to wobble.

"Piper!" Paige shouted, running to catch her

sister before she fell. Phoebe turned at Paige's cry and joined her. Just as they reached Piper, she began to pitch forward. Paige caught her wrist, and Phoebe got a handful of the white robe she wore, and together they kept her from tumbling off the edge of a thirty-foot cliff.

"Piper, are you okay?" Phoebe asked as they sat her down on the damp grass away from the edge. "What happened?"

"Fine, I'm fine," Piper answered, still sounding like she was not altogether there. "No big."

"Yes big," Paige declared. She was still trembling from the momentary fright and the rush of adrenaline that followed it. "Piper, you almost fell."

"Almost, but I didn't," Piper said. "Can we go home now?"

"Soon," Phoebe replied. "We just have to finish something up."

"I'm finished," Piper insisted. "I'll see you at home." She started to lurch to her feet, but Phoebe pushed her back down.

"You just stay there, Piper," she said.

Piper looked at her in an off-kilter way. "You pushed me."

"That's right, and I'll do it again," Phoebe said, increasingly alarmed by her sister's condition.

Paige recognized Phoebe's tough-chick voice. "I wouldn't mess with her, Piper," she warned.

Piper turned her dreamy gaze on Paige. "I can take her. Been working out."

"No joke," Paige answered.

Phoebe gripped Paige's shoulder, hard enough to hurt. "Let's do it," she said. "Now."

"I'm with ya, sis," Paige replied. This had definitely gone on too long. Digging into the pocket of the pants she wore under her robe, she pulled out the spell she had written earlier and rose, standing next to Phoebe so they could both read it in the moonlight.

> *Magic forces on this rise,*
> *Piper needs no exercise,*
> *Lift whatever spell she's under,*
> *Lest the Charmed Ones be put asunder.*

The air around Piper seemed to shimmer for a moment, her very form becoming indistinct, as if she were surrounded by honey or molasses. But then she came back into focus, blinking and rubbing at her eyes like someone just waking up from a long sleep. "What's going on?" she asked. Her voice sounded like the old Piper, too. "What are we doing here? For that matter, where is— are we on Corona Heights?"

Phoebe and Paige caught each other's glances and traded smiles. Piper was back! "That's right," Phoebe said. "Third-night-after-solstice ritual. Reconnecting with the earth."

"Did I . . . I feel strange," Piper said.

"You almost fainted," Paige told her, leaving out the rest of it. "We caught you."

"Oh. Well, thanks," Piper said. She didn't sound completely convinced. "Are we finished? It's a little cold here."

She was right, a cool breeze had come up while they'd been here, and even though the day had been warm, evenings were never exactly balmy in San Francisco.

"Sure," Phoebe said. "We're done. Paige, you want to take us home?"

Paige felt relieved to have her oldest sister back among them. They hadn't completely finished the ritual they'd come here for, but that was probably okay. It was mostly a symbolic thing, anyway, and she hadn't been getting that much out of it. Now that Piper seemed back to normal, she felt as if a great weight had been lifted from her shoulders, and everything else paled in importance. "Sure," she agreed happily. "Let's go home."

Chapter
6

Phoebe was awakened by music booming up through the floorboards of her room. She glanced at the clock beside her bed. Six o'clock. In the morning. Tugging on a silk robe over her tank top and pajama pants, she stormed downstairs and threw open the living room door.

Inside, she found Piper spread out on the floor, touching her toes. "Piper!" Phoebe snapped. "What are you doing?"

Piper beamed up at her. "Good morning, Phoebes," she said, the very picture of slightly-out-of-breath cheerfulness. "How are you today?"

"How am I? The question is, how are you? I thought you were over this last night."

Piper turned her attention back to the TV. "Over what?"

Phoebe snatched the remote off the floor and lowered the volume. She felt let down, disappointed—she had been convinced the spell they had performed had fixed whatever was going on with Piper. Apparently, though, the fix had only been temporary. "The neighbors are complaining about the noise," she said. "And I don't mean the neighbors next door. I mean the ones in Nevada."

"I have to *feel* the beat," Piper explained, grabbing her leg and bending forward until her forehead touched her knee. "It's not enough to hear the music, I have to let it fill me."

"Why, Piper? You look great. You're in perfect health. What do you need this for?"

Piper didn't speak until she had raised her forehead from her other knee. "I'm just trying to be my ideal me," she said. "I'm trying to regain my lost confidence by being the best self I can be."

"What I don't understand," Paige said from behind Phoebe, "is how she can even say that junk with a straight face."

Phoebe hadn't heard Paige come in—and that was with the volume turned down. *Maybe I've already suffered permanent hearing loss,* she thought. *This has got to end.* She clenched her hands into fists and called as loud as she could. "Leo!"

Leo orbed in a moment later, glistening wet, a towel wrapped around his waist. "This couldn't wait three minutes for me to get some clothes on?"

"She's your wife," Phoebe said, gesturing toward Piper. "What do you think?"

Leo grimaced. "I thought you said you had removed the spell last night."

"We thought we did," Paige put in. "Looks like we were wrong."

"Apparently," Leo agreed. "But I've checked her out. So far, there's no harmful effect from all the exercise. I can't see that there's much beneficial effect either. She's limber, and she's toned, but she's not building muscle mass."

"If it's not doing anything, she should give it a rest," Phoebe suggested, shouting over the blaring TV, hoping Piper would take the hint. But Piper just kept stretching and jumping and annoying everyone around her.

"I guess we'd better figure this out," Paige said. "Before she keels over or one of us has to tranquilize her to make her stop."

Learning that they hadn't counteracted whatever spell Piper suffered under agonized Phoebe. Piper had spent a lifetime helping out her little sister—sure, they'd saved each other's life many times over now, but the bond that connected them went way beyond that.

She remembered a time when she was five or six, and terrified of going to sleep in the dark because of the ghosts or monsters that might be hiding around her room. Ironic, considering the varied and horrific creatures she'd battled since then, but in those days, of course, she'd only known a small child's innate fear of what lurks in the darkness.

She had complained to Prue, their oldest sister, about her fears and asked how Prue dealt with the ghosts and other creatures that haunted her room. Prue—teasing, Phoebe understood now, if not then—pointed to a china ballerina statue on her nightstand that Phoebe had long admired. "She watches out for me, and chases them away," Prue told her. Phoebe had been amazed that such a simple statue could perform such a crucial task, but she believed her big sister's every utterance.

Two troubled nights later, Prue went for a sleepover at the home of one of her girlfriends. Phoebe took advantage of the opportunity to sneak into her room and borrow her ballerina statue, just for the night, to see if it would protect her as it did Prue. It seemed to work—that night, with the ballerina next to her own bed, she drifted off into blissful slumber, untroubled by any night terrors. All was well until early morning, when she reached for a glass of water on her night table and knocked the ballerina onto the floor. It shattered, and Phoebe knew she'd be in serious trouble when Prue came home.

But Piper, middle sister and peacekeeper, came to her rescue. She accepted full responsibility for having liberated the ballerina from Prue's room and leaving it in Phoebe's, thereby taking the brunt of Prue's fury when she got home and found her statue in the trash. Phoebe still shared the blame—she had, after all, broken it—but Piper's involvement dissipated it. Best of all, Piper did it without Phoebe asking her to, and she never held it over her younger sister, never reminding her of it again. Some sisters, Phoebe was sure, would have said "Hey, remember the ballerina?" anytime conflict came between them. But not Piper—it was just something she could do for her baby sister, and she did it.

Phoebe had never forgotten it, or any of the other innumerable kindnesses Piper had done for her. She tried to pay Piper back, but knew that a lifetime of effort couldn't fully discharge the debt she owed. So at a moment like this, when Piper was in trouble, the pressure Phoebe felt to help her was a physical ache. She didn't know what she could do, but she had to do something.

Phoebe drew Paige out of the room so they could hear each other over Piper's video. "Is there anything helpful in your professor's book?" she asked. "We need to find out what's going on around here."

Paige scrunched up her face. "Not really. *The Visitors* is pretty boring reading. I've been trying to get through it, but man, the guy could put an insomniac to sleep."

"Well, what does he say about UFOs?" Phoebe pressed. "He must have some ideas."

"He's full of ideas," Paige replied. "That's what the whole thing is. But a lot of it is just the usual stuff. The universe is filled with billions and billions of stars, and each star has a whole solar system around it, which means more billions and billions of potentially inhabited planets. We don't know exactly how old the universe is, but if the big bang theory is true, then solar systems farther out toward the edges are much older than ours, which means that civilizations, if they exist, have had more time to develop faster-than-light travel. So maybe they're visiting us. Only what I just said in two sentences he takes about six chapters to conclude, complete with footnotes. And diagrams."

"And none of that explains why people would be suddenly drawn to Meg Winship exercise videos," Phoebe added, trying to ignore the sound of Piper's pounding through the walls. "Or what the connection might be between somebody who was supposedly abducted, like Daphne Bodine, or Piper, who as far as we know has never been on a flying saucer."

"It was weird," Paige said. "When I was at the professor's home, I couldn't get him to open up at all. So I did a little trick for him, orbed one of his books, hoping that it would make him think I was, you know, one of the aliens. I thought he'd be so happy that I was real. But instead, it seemed to totally freak him out. He couldn't wait to get rid of me after that."

"You showed him your power?" Phoebe asked, astonished at Paige. She'd gotten in trouble for that kind of thing before. "Are you crazy?"

"I knew how he'd take it, Phoebe. It would never occur to him that I'm a witch. He thought I was part of an advanced race with technology he's never seen. He just didn't react the way I expected."

Phoebe thought it over for a moment. *Done's done,* she realized. *And there don't seem to be any repercussions, so let's move on.* "Okay," she said. "Why don't you keep reading and see if you can learn anything else?"

"I might try visiting him again," Paige suggested. "See if I can get him to summarize some of it for me so I don't have to keep fighting off a coma."

"Okay, but if you do, be careful. You've already frightened the poor man, apparently. You don't want to spook him too much."

And while you're doing that, she thought, *I'll be finding out what's so special about Meg Winship.*

Dr. Carter Haywood punched the numbers on his telephone with trembling fingers. He held the handpiece to his ear and listened to it ring, torn between wanting it to be answered and hoping it wouldn't be. After the third ring, someone picked up.

"Ideal You Enterprises," a cheerful female voice said.

"M-Meg Winship, please."

"I'm sorry, Ms. Winship is unavailable. Would you like to leave a message?"

What message could I leave? Dr. Haywood wondered. "It's very urgent," he pressed.

"I'm terribly sorry," the voice said. It had lost some of its cheer but was still crisp and professional. "Ms. Winship is extremely busy, and is not accepting any calls at all until after her upcoming rally."

"I understand that. But . . . just please ask her to call Dr. Carter Haywood. As soon as she possibly can."

There seemed to be a different note in the woman's voice when she replied. "Dr. Carter Haywood?"

"That's right," he said.

"Just a moment, please."

So his name *did* mean something to her. Even after all this time. With grateful anticipation, he waited for her to come on the line.

Meg Winship hung up the phone, disappointed. Haywood should have been her greatest supporter. But he was too cowardly, to afraid to learn the truth of his own theories. Instead of being a booster, he had become a doomsayer, a worrywart. He had believed that he was warning her. "You're going too far," he'd said. "You don't know what you're getting yourself into."

She smiled. She knew precisely what she was getting into. She was fully aware—more aware than she had ever been, or than most people would ever be in their lives. *Knowledge breeds knowledge,* she thought. Once she had taken Haywood's ideas to their logical conclusions, she had learned that they were only the beginning. What he had seen as answers were only more questions. But she had been able to figure out the next question, and the next.

And, unlike him, she had discovered whom to ask.

That made all the difference.

With the knowledge she gained came power— not the power she ultimately sought, but power that would lead her toward that greater goal. It protected her, and enabled her to amass yet more power. Dr. Haywood—if he had been stronger— would have been proud. But he'd turned out to be a weak man, after all. Frightened.

And, unfortunately, beyond her immediate control.

Meg knew that she could manipulate women. For lack of a better word, she thought of her power as a kind of hypnosis, but it didn't require that her subjects remain asleep, or in a trancelike state. And her control, once she had exercised it, was nearly total—she could make any woman under her influence do anything at all, no matter how awful or upsetting she would have found it before.

But she couldn't extend that power to men. Fortunately, in most instances, she didn't need to. She would attain her goals with the help of the city's female population, and the men would fall in line when the time came. She would have liked Dr. Haywood to join her effort, but she didn't need him to.

There were other ways to deal with him.

She pressed the "Intercom" button on her phone and called for Sasha. Sasha would put things in motion. She knew how to do that kind of thing.

Dr. Haywood might become a problem. Most likely, if he spoke up against her, he would be branded a maniac. His academic career would be recalled, his disgrace remembered, and he would be ignored.

But he was a loose end she didn't want to have dangling out there. Just in case.

She waited for almost two minutes—Sasha never took longer than that, as long as she was on the premises. When one minute and fifty seconds had passed, Sasha showed up in her doorway. "You called for me?"

Meg nodded, jotted down Carter Haywood's name on a slip of paper, and pushed it across her desk. Sasha picked it up, read it, nodded. She understood, then. To make sure, Meg lit a candle on her desk. The smell of vanilla filled the air.

Sasha held the slip of paper to the candle's flame, not letting go even when the fire licked at her fingers. "Consider it done," she said. "Will that be all?"

"Yes, Sasha," Meg said, pleased at her control over such a strong-willed woman. "That's all."

Sasha turned and left the office, walking smartly and with purpose.

Meg knew she wouldn't have to worry about Carter Haywood at all.

"Thanks for meeting me, Bill." Phoebe put down her drink to shake his hand. Not wanting to go to the *Bay Mirror's* office, she'd called him and asked him to join her at the same out-of-the-way coffee shop in which she'd read through the city's tabloids. No one knew her here, and she had realized she really liked the white-chocolate mocha, even in its low-fat variety. This time, she left the hat and shades home, but wore her hair slicked close to her scalp, a vintage silk-screened tee, and bleached denim jeans with frayed edges over Ugg boots, which were surprisingly cool on warm days.

Bill Conason glanced at the vintage photos on the walls as he sat down across from her. He had already ordered a drink, and he placed it on the table. "Nice place," he said. "City sure looked different in those days."

Phoebe nodded, but didn't want to get involved in a long discussion of the effects of the 1906 earthquake. "I'm sorry for the secrecy," she said. "I didn't want to go into the office today, but I wanted to talk to you about UFOs some more."

He chuckled and took a long sip from his coffee. "I think I told you everything I know, Phoebe."

She didn't buy that for a second. "You were right, you know. I checked the tabloids. Lots of activity, lots of people reporting strange objects, and even some abductions. And you said many of those people have reported it to the *Bay Mirror* too. You must have their names, contact information. I'd like to talk to some of them."

"You know that's a story we're not going to run," he warned her. "Not unless there's some huge break, like a mass sighting or proof positive. And the tabloids already have it, so you can't sell it there. What are you going to do with it?"

"Let's just say I have personal reasons and leave it at that." Phoebe read the look on his face. "I'm not going to try to sell it as a story," she assured him. "And if I come up with anything newsworthy, I'll bring it to you."

He took another drink from his cup, and put it down on the table. "Have you seen something?" he asked. "Is that what this is about?"

Phoebe couldn't restrain a laugh. "No, no," she said. "It's not that. Like I said, I have a personal reason for wanting to talk to some of these witnesses, but it isn't that. Will you get me some names?"

Bill considered her request for a long moment, then slowly nodded. "Give me your home e-mail address," he said. "I'll send them over when I get back to the office. You sure you're not going to write a book or something?"

"I swear," Phoebe said. She wrote down her e-mail address on the back of her coffee receipt and slid it across the table to him. He pocketed it quickly. "That's not what it's about at all."

"And if you reach the point that you can talk about these 'personal reasons,' you'll come to me?"

"I promise."

"Okay." He drained his cup and rose. "Check your e-mail."

She thanked him, and they left the coffee shop, going their separate ways at the corner. He'd be back at work in twenty minutes, she knew. She would be at the computer in twenty-one, waiting for those names.

Chapter 7

Paige pounded on the door of Dr. Haywood's house. She had tried the doorbell first, but if it worked, she couldn't hear anything. And since there had been no response, she had to assume that it didn't. Finally, after knocking for more than a minute, she heard noises from inside: a crash, and then the shuffling of feet. While she waited, two women jogged past the house. Like the other joggers she had seen in the neighborhood, these wore headphones connected to portable CD players at their waists.

"What is it?" Dr. Haywood demanded grumpily when he opened the door, looking more drawn and pale than he had the other day. He blinked a couple of times behind his thick lenses. "Oh, Paige. It's you."

His voice sounded strange when he said it,

giving Paige the impression that he was disappointed, that perhaps he'd been expecting someone else. *But maybe it's more that I still scare him,*
she thought, again feeling a pang of guilt over
her deception. "Can I come in, Dr. Haywood?"

He glanced behind himself, as if the answer
to her question was back there somewhere.
"Well . . . is it important?" he asked. "You know
I'm a very busy person."

"I appreciate that, Dr. Haywood, really," she
assured him. "I just . . . I had a few more questions. About your theories."

"I would think that if there's anyone who
doesn't need to hear my pathetic theories, it
would be you, Ms. Matthews."

Time to come clean, Paige thought. *Well, almost.*
"Yeah, about that," she said. "I might have been
just the teensiest bit dishonest. About what
I am."

"I saw what you did with my own eyes, Paige.
You don't need to hide anything from me."

"I know that," she said. "It's just . . . what I
am may not be exactly what you think I am. But
I can't tell you what I really am."

"Look . . . why don't you come in, but only
for a minute or two. I really can't spare the time
to chat with you today." Dr. Haywood was on
edge, almost frantic. He chewed his lower lip,
tugged at his gray hair with one hand. Paige had
never seen him quite so anxious.

She followed him into the house, which hadn't

changed since her last visit. Knowing she was coming back here, she had worn gray this time, cotton-spandex pants with plenty of zippers and a charcoal scoop-neck top. "I wouldn't ask if it wasn't really important."

"It is important, vitally important," he said.

Lost me already, she thought. *How could he know?* "What do—"

"She's fooling with things she doesn't understand," he went on. He turned in circles in the middle of his front room, threatening nearby piles of books with every rotation. "And she's got to be stopped before it's too late."

"Dr. Haywood," Paige said, hoping to tether him to the earth again. "Can we just—"

Once more, he cut her off. "Paige, if you aren't one of them, then you've got to help. You must help me . . . help all of us."

"I'll do whatever I can," Paige promised, although she had no idea what it was she was supposed to help with. Dr. Haywood was bordering on panic, it seemed. She'd have to calm him down before he would be able to make any sense at all. "Why don't I start by making us some tea?" she suggested. "Then we can sit down and talk about all of this. Rationally."

"Yes, fine, tea. Whatever you say. It's just . . ." He trailed off, tugging at his own hair again. Paige worried about his health. *If he gets himself worked up more, he'll be in stroke territory*, she thought. She went past him, into his kitchen. She didn't really know if tea would help or not, but if it gave him something to do with his hands, distracted him momentarily from whatever was driving him into a frenzy, then it couldn't hurt. She didn't see a teapot but she found a cooking pot, ran some water into it, and put it on the stove to boil while she searched the cupboards for tea.

Predictably, his organizational skills were the same in here as in the rest of the house. There was a box of tea bags in a deep drawer with assorted silverware and utensils and the front page of the *Bay Mirror* from April 11, 1989. At a glance, she couldn't see anything especially pertinent on that day's newspaper, and figured he had just set it in the drawer and forgotten about it.

When the water reached a boil, she took it off the heat and poured it over tea bags into two cups. "Dr. Haywood," she called. "Do you use sugar or cream?"

There was no answer, but she heard him shuffling around in the other room. Then she heard the front door open. "Dr. Haywood?" she repeated. Again, no answer came.

She left the cups where they were and went back to the front room. It was empty, but the front door was ajar. Paige stepped out onto the front porch.

It took her a moment to spot him, because she was looking for someone standing up, and he was lying down. In the brown, dry grass of his front yard. Facedown. "Dr. Haywood!" she shouted, running to his side. "Are you . . . ?"

She touched his shoulder. He didn't respond, didn't move. She turned his head. His eyes were open, but stared at her blindly. When she shifted him back, she saw that his shirt had two jagged rips in it, soaked with blood, and more had pooled in the grass underneath him.

Her backpack was in the house. She ran back inside, grabbed it, fished her cell phone out, and dialed 911. It was only after she had done so that she realized she hadn't seen anyone around who might have done this to poor Dr. Haywood. When she had come outside, the only people she had spotted, jogging off into the distance, had been the same two women with the headphones and CD players that she'd seen upon her arrival.

"I guess it's a good thing I caught the case," Darryl Morris said. They were standing on the street outside Dr. Haywood's house. Crime scene investigators in coveralls were searching the lawn on hands and knees, bagging everything but the dead grass. Others were working inside the house.

"I should have asked for you," Paige admitted. "But I was kind of freaked out, you know?"

"You've seen worse," Darryl said flatly.

"True," she said. "But it's usually preceded by some creepy demon, so I'm prepared. This is just . . ." Paige found it hard to continue.

"Murder?" Darryl finished her thought. "So

you're telling me there's no magical connection?"

"I came here to talk to him about something we're looking into," Paige answered. "But he went outside while I was making tea. I don't know why. I didn't hear anyone come to the door, and he didn't say anything. He just went out, and then I went out to look for him, and that's how I found him."

"And what are the chances that you'll tell me what you're looking into?"

Paige thought about that for a moment. "Umm, slim to none?"

"That's what I thought," Darryl said. "I was thinking about calling you guys the other day. Had a guy in, complaining that his wife had been abducted by aliens, and I thought it was right up your alley."

She let that sink in. It was possible that the case wasn't connected with the other so-called abductions they were working on, or with Piper's condition. But just barely. "I don't suppose his wife was drawn to workout tapes after her abduction, by any chance?"

Darryl's jaw dropped open so fast, she almost broke out laughing. If she wasn't surrounded by homicide investigators, she probably would have. "Paige," he said tersely. "How do you know that?"

"Just call it a hunch," she replied.

Darryl shook his head rapidly. "Give me something," he demanded. "This is related, isn't it?"

"It might be," she admitted. "It's hard to know for sure." She told him, briefly, about Phoebe's reader and her sister, and Dr. Haywood's past—and the fact that he had been fired from U.C. Berkeley for his UFO theories. "I came to him because I needed a lesson on UFOs," she explained, pointedly omitting Piper from the discussion. "What they might be, and how they might be affecting people."

"And this is all because of a letter Phoebe got at the paper?"

"Yeah, that's what started it."

He eyed her distrustfully. "You're not leaving out anything I should know?"

At least he had given her an out by the way he phrased the question. "Nope," she said. "Nothing you should know. But if you find out anything, please give me a call. Especially anything involving UFOs or someone named Meg Winship."

He started to say something else, but then caught himself and dropped it. Paige was glad. She didn't want to have to lie to him. Better to just answer his questions with the least possible detail and let him wonder.

When she left him there, he looked like he was still wondering.

Bill Conason wanted a big story.

More than that, he needed a big story.

People were getting their news from TV and

the Internet. Newspapers, nearly all of which were now owned by multinational entertainment conglomerates, were cutting staff to maximize profits. The *Bay Mirror* was no different, he feared. One of these days, the stockholders would want to see profits boosted, and the pink slips would start to show up. When that happened, the reporters who were household names, or the ones with Pulitzer Prizes under their belts, would be the ones who stayed.

The ones who filed small stories, on time, week in and week out, would be asked to go.

That's what Bill Conason was, he knew. Dependable. Steady. His editor knew he could be counted on to dig up the facts, to get the quotes right, to analyze the details of the story.

But that kind of reporting no longer cut it. Bill understood that. A reporter had to make a splash now and then. And it had been far too long since he'd made a splash.

There were plenty of splashy stories in the city this week. The bodies south of Market were big news, and much of Metro's staff was on it. A big story, but a story to which he had not been assigned.

Now, though . . . now, he thought he was onto something. Phoebe Halliwell had a story on the line, he was sure of it. The UFO bit was crazy, but there was something to it—at least, something to the fact that so many people seemed to believe in it, all of a sudden.

He'd sent her the list of names he'd promised. She would check them out. And he'd make sure to stay in touch, to find out what she learned when she investigated them. Let her do the legwork, then he'd snake the story out from under her.

He was the reporter, after all. She was a smart young woman, easy on the eyes, and people opened up to her. But he was the one who could string words into sentences. He'd take her raw material and make it into front page news.

He'd make a splash.

Phoebe took the list of names that Bill sent her and started at the top. Interestingly, although both men and women had made the reports, it seemed that the only people who had apparently been abducted were women. She wasn't sure what that might mean, but she was determined to find out.

The first name on the list was Frieda Westen, who lived on Telegraph Hill, a couple of blocks from the bay. Phoebe drove to her apartment and knocked on the door. A minute later, it was opened by a harried-looking young man with dark, curly hair and weary eyes. "Yes?" he said.

"I'm here about Frieda Westen," Phoebe explained. She flashed her press credentials, even though she wasn't acting in her official capacity.

The young man barely glanced at it. "What about her?"

Phoebe could already hear the familiar beat of a Meg Winship video. "She's been working out a lot, hasn't she? Since the abduction."

The guy nodded and swallowed. "A whole lot."

"Look," Phoebe said sympathetically. "I know what you're going through. I'm trying to help. Can I see her for a minute?" In fact, she wasn't certain what she hoped to accomplish. But she felt that by investigating enough of the victims, she might be able to find some kind of common thread. Since nothing else had worked, maybe that thread would lead to a solution. Anything was worth a try, at this point.

The young man wiggled his shoulders. "I guess," he said. "Sure, if you want."

"Thanks," Phoebe said. He led her into the apartment, which was furnished in a tastefully minimalist, modern style. From the living room's huge windows there was a bay view. This was an expensive piece of real estate.

Inside, the music was loud, but Phoebe was getting used to that. Nor was she surprised to find Frieda outfitted in workout clothes, exercising in front of a wall-mounted plasma-screen TV that showed Meg Winship's video with crystal clarity.

"Frieda!" the young man shouted. She looked up from her efforts. "This is . . . I'm sorry, what's your name?"

Phoebe took it from there, stepping forward with her hand extended. Frieda, young and pretty and obviously fit, reached up reflexively from her position on the floor and shook it. The moment their skin touched skin, Phoebe was shaken by a vision. An array of lights skidded past below her, whirling frenetically. It was only after Phoebe let Frieda's hand go that she realized what she had seen—the city of San Francisco, as if observed from a very fast helicopter or low-flying plane.

Phoebe blew out the breath she had been inadvertently holding. "Hi," she said. "My name is Phoebe Halliwell. I understand you had a strange experience recently."

"That's what Frank says." Frieda shook her head, causing her tight blond curls to vibrate. "I don't know anything about it."

"And do you know why you've been driven to exercise with Meg Winship?" Phoebe asked.

"Well, it's good for me," Frieda replied quickly. "I'm becoming my ideal me."

"Maybe you already were your ideal you," Phoebe suggested gently. "Has that occurred to you?"

Frieda shook her head again, this time more decisively. "No, there was room for improvement," she said. "But I'm getting there."

Phoebe started to say something else, but Frieda's eyes were already locked on the screen again, and she was taking her position for a different exercise. Phoebe looked at Frank, who shrugged once more. "This is the way she's been," he said. "Ever since it happened. Do you think it's bad for her?"

"It's not good," Phoebe stated.

Phoebe went to another home after that, and another, working her way down the list. In each one, she found the same story. Loud Meg Winship videos, accompanied by exercise to the point of exhaustion. These women worked out all day, sleeping only in fits when they collapsed on their exercise mats.

More ominously, she thought, along the way she saw numerous posters and handbills—glued to walls, newspaper boxes, tucked under windshield wipers, and elsewhere—advertising Meg Winship's coming rally. And everywhere she went she saw women jogging with headphones on. She couldn't help suspecting that they were *all* listening to Meg Winship. Somehow the Winship cult had reached epidemic proportions with nobody noticing. It wasn't just Piper and Daphne Bodine she and Paige had to rescue. It was hundreds of women, maybe thousands of them, all over San Francisco.

The idea made a shiver of fear run up Phoebe's back. She hoped she and Paige were up to the job. Because it didn't look like the Power of Three would be an option this time.

When the video ended, Piper decided it was time for a change of scenery. She had been working hard, improving herself, creating her own ideal her. Her self-confidence had been strengthened along with her muscles. But she'd been doing it alone, and there were times, she thought, that sisterhood was called for.

After tying her hair back in a ponytail and changing into a sleeveless, ribbed crewneck top, slightly flared yoga pants, and white track shoes, she headed out the door. She knew there was a Meg Winship audio CD out there somewhere that she could listen to as she ran. But she wasn't even sure she needed it. Meg's voice echoed in her head, Meg's signature music reverberated through her bones.

The skies over San Francisco were blue and virtually cloudless, the sun that splashed the city warm and welcoming. Piper loved her native city, but the one thing that wore on her from time to time was the weather. Gray, overcast, or foggy most of the time, she missed seeing the sun, sometimes for weeks at a stretch. The winters were hard, not because it turned cold, though it did, but because it was easy to forget that spring would bring blue skies and warm days again. As she jogged today, she reveled in the sunshine on her cheeks and forehead. *A little SPF 45 would have been a good idea,* she thought, but going back home and putting some on didn't enter her mind.

After she had run about eight blocks she saw a house—a typical San Francisco row house, with white walls and red trim and flowers thriving in a window box. Piper had never been to that house, had no idea who lived there. But she was drawn to it. She jogged up to the door, rang the bell, and then ran in place as she waited for an answer. From inside, she heard familiar music.

A young lady with strawberry blond hair, wearing a yellow leotard and red running shorts, opened the door. She was running in place on the other side. "Hi," she said happily. "I'm April."

"I'm Piper," Piper replied, just as cheerfully. "Good to meet you. Want to run?"

"Sure," April said. "Just let me get my CD player."

Moments later, they were jogging together down the block. April spotted a Meg Winship rally poster tacked to the plywood shielding a construction site, and pointed it out to Piper. "You going?" she asked.

"Of course," Piper replied. "Wouldn't miss it!"

"Same here," April said. They ran along in silence for another couple of blocks, until they saw two women jogging across the street before them.

"Hey!" Piper called. The two stopped and jogged in place, waiting for them to catch up. When Piper and April reached them, they all introduced themselves, and ran up the hill together.

Piper was making friends right and left. *Turns out it's easy to make friends,* she thought, *when you are your ideal you.*

Nothing to it at all.

Chapter

8

Darryl had come to think of the Charmed Ones as family, but all families had their squabbles, and this case was about to start one. *Sometimes—no, make that most of the time—those women are trouble,* Darryl thought. *Trouble with a capital T and that rhymes with P and that stands for Piper, Phoebe, and Paige, any of them, or all three together.* Sure, they had saved the city from dangers he would have had no clue how to cope with. And they'd helped him out from time to time. But they played havoc with his clearance rate, because cases in which they were involved often went down on the books as unsolved. Since the perpetrators were not your run-of-the-mill criminals, the Charmed Ones usually "vanquished" them, to use their jargon. And there was no box to check on the police forms for that. So Darryl was constantly on the edge of trouble—closing some major cases, but then leaving more officially unsolved than any other detective in the department.

So when he'd seen Paige at the Haywood crime scene, a headache had started to build that extended to the corners of his jaw. He'd finally fought his way clear of the last batch of paperwork and caught a new case, and a Charmed One had beaten him to it. She'd been at the scene when Dr. Haywood had been murdered, although she swore she hadn't seen anything. He believed her—Paige was no liar. The only people she had seen in the vicinity had been some female joggers. She had given him a description, though it was vague, and he'd sent some uniformed officers to scour the neighborhood for them. But they'd come back within twenty minutes, discouraged. Women were jogging in pairs and groups all over the city— Darryl knew that was true because he'd seen at least two dozen of them on his way to the Haywood house—and without more to go on, there was no way to isolate the ones Paige had only half-noticed.

Which made things more difficult, but didn't bring the investigation to a halt. There were only so many reasons an old man would be stabbed to death. The nature of the murder made it seem like an acquaintance crime—a friend or neighbor, with some powerful emotion driving them. A random murderer would have been less likely to stab, and the killing would have been done in conjunction with some other crime, like robbery. That hadn't been the case here. The man had been stabbed, quietly and efficiently, in the few moments between when Paige heard him go outside and the time she got there.

And the fact that Haywood went outside at all supported his theory. Unless he had just stepped out for his mail or a newspaper or something, he probably would not have done so had there not been someone he knew summoning him. If a stranger was out there, he'd have been more likely to call out to Paige before he went, or to stay at the door and talk from there. He was an old man, frail, and probably not especially prone to taking chances with his physical well-being. A knife-wielding person in his yard, or even just a stranger with a concealed knife, would have spurred him to caution, not carelessness.

Darryl walked back into the house—not quite one of those overstuffed firetraps that crazy people sometimes lived in, but on the way to becoming one—nodding to the uniformed officer guarding the door. The officer, middle-aged and with a paunch that threatened to overlap his belt, gave him a casual nod in return. "Not as bad as some, is it?" he said.

The comment brought Darryl up short. "What do you mean?"

"Well, you know. Stabbing's usually a pretty messy way to do it. This one, though, it's pretty clean. Yard soaked up most of it, right?"

Darryl fixed the officer with an angry glare. "Dr. Haywood is a person," he pointed out. "Unfortunately deceased, but a person nonetheless, and deserving of your respect. Particularly at this moment."

The big cop wilted under his stare. "Yeah . . . yes, sir. Sorry, sir. Guess I let myself lose sight of that sometimes."

"Don't let it happen again," Darryl said. He brushed past the man and went inside. The cop was right—it looked like Haywood never watered his lawn; except for fog, that blood was probably the only liquid it had tasted in months. *But still, you don't say that kind of thing out loud.*

The acquaintance theory still made the most sense to Darryl. The hard part would be figuring out who knew the ex-professor, and who might have something against him worth killing over. In most homes, there would be an address book, usually in a desk or near a telephone. In this one, though, Darryl couldn't even spot the phone. And there were so many books that trying to find one small address book would be worse than looking for a needle in a haystack—it would be more like seeking out one particular piece of hay among all the rest.

The crime scene investigators had pretty much given up on the inside already. There was no indication that whoever killed Dr. Haywood had been in the house, and based on Paige's

account, Haywood had definitely stepped outside to meet his assailant. They had combed the
area around the doorway carefully, tagging and
bagging everything they'd found, from stray
pieces of lint to hairs to a piece of a cracker
wedged in the corner. The doorjamb still showed
the fine powder used to reveal fingerprints. The
real crime scene, though, had been determined to
be the front yard. Footprints had been identified
in the dirt—female, relatively small, athletic
shoes, which supported Paige's story of the joggers—and Haywood's death had been almost
instantaneous. Whoever had driven the knife
into him had known what she was doing. Most
stabbing victims died slowly, as the lifeblood
trickled from their body, but his heart had been
ruptured and he'd fallen at once, bleeding out in
just moments.

Left alone in the house, Darryl tried to find a
starting point, an angle from which to consider
Dr. Carter Haywood's life and death. Paige had
been vague about why she had come here, but it
had to do with UFOs and some investigation
she and her sisters were working on. And somehow it tied into workout videos, which was a
leap of logic that he couldn't quite make. But
the guy who had come in to file a complaint
about his abducted wife—Mr. Haas—had said
that when he came home and found her, she'd
been exercising to a video that he didn't know
she owned. And Paige had mentioned Meg

Winship, whose name Darryl knew from her popular books and videos, as well as the ubiquitous posters advertising her upcoming rally. She had also told him about Dr. Haywood's dismissal from U.C. Berkeley over his insistence that UFOs were real.

All of which made UFOs seem like the obvious starting point. But having reached that conclusion, Darryl started poking around in the books that covered nearly every surface, and found that at least half of them were about UFOs. He had no idea so many books on the subject existed. *How could all these people write about something for which there's not a scintilla of hard evidence?* he wondered. But then, he had always been a practical man, as most detectives were. He hadn't even wanted to believe the Halliwells were witches until it had been proven to him beyond a shadow of a doubt.

Darryl tried to stay relatively well informed. Another hallmark of a good detective—he might need to make connections between disparate ideas at any point, and the more he knew about the world around him, the easier that would be. So he knew the basics about UFOs. There had been sightings throughout recorded history, but the real hysteria hadn't come about until after the first reported sighting in the United States, in the late 1940s. Most sightings could be easily explained away: weather balloons, kites, bright stars, methane gas, unusual cloud formations.

But not all were so simply dismissed. The United States Air Force had spent decades investigating UFOs, in a classified report called Project Blue Book. The report had concluded that UFOs did not constitute a threat to national security, but it had not successfully explained what they were. UFO theorists pointed to "evidence" of alien encounters in Roswell, New Mexico, and the remote Nevada military installation referred to as "Area 51." Roswell, in particular, had been the scene of a widely reported UFO crash, and the military there announced that they'd recovered pieces of a flying saucer. Very quickly, Darryl remembered, they'd changed their story, claiming that it had, in fact, been a weather balloon and not a saucer at all.

So people—some reputable, others not so much—had been seeing strange objects in the skies for centuries, and with increasing frequency in the last several decades. That made sense, Darryl thought, when one considered that since the latter half of the twentieth century, the world's population had boomed, so there were simply more people and therefore fewer events would go unwitnessed.

Darryl himself was not a believer in UFOs, but until about six years ago, he hadn't believed in magic, either. So who knew what was possible? He was determined to keep an open mind. But he would need some scientific proof, or at least the evidence of his own senses, before he would conclusively agree that extraterrestrial visitors existed.

Which led to one possible theory of Dr. Haywood's death. He had, according to Paige, trumpeted the existence of UFOs for years. If he was on the verge of some kind of breakthrough, of being able to prove his theories, and if the extraterrestrials themselves were aware of this and felt threatened, they might have killed him to silence him.

Darryl chuckled softly. That was a theory to keep in his vest pocket—well, metaphorically, at least, since he didn't wear a vest—but not one to share with the department brass. It wasn't one that he could proceed on, but something to keep at the back of his mind as he looked for a more mundane solution to the crime.

Leaving the downstairs behind, he climbed up to the second floor and found Dr. Haywood's bedroom. More of the same. Haywood seemed to scratch notes on any slip of paper available, from receipts to the envelope for his water bill to the back of a postcard from his eye doctor reminding him to make an appointment. The notes were meaningless to anyone but Dr. Haywood himself, Darryl concluded after several minutes of study. He couldn't translate "74 mim docs 323=txt," which he found scrawled on the margin of a newspaper's advertising supplement, but at least he could read the letters and numbers. On many of the other notes, he couldn't even make that much headway.

The books here were pretty much the same as those downstairs, as well. Books on UFOs, some on other paranormal subjects, and others on topics ranging from philosophy to physics. All non-fiction, or at least presented as such. There were even books on the bed itself, though only covering half of it, presumably leaving the other half available for Haywood to sleep on.

It was when Darryl examined these that he found what he considered to be the most telling item so far—a book called *The Winship Way*, written by one Meg Winship. He laughed out loud when he spotted it, then silenced himself before the uniformed cop downstairs heard him. Drawing it from its place beneath a stack of other titles, he looked at the picture on the cover: Meg Winship in workout gear, fit and healthy.

It seemed a strange book for someone like Haywood to own, though. He didn't seem to exercise, and at his age and general condition, one of Winship's workouts would probably have been fatal. Darryl flipped the book open and on the title page, saw a handwritten inscription.

"To my favorite prof," it said, "Carter Haywood, mentor and friend." Below that was a signature that was unmistakably Meg Winship's.

Now, Darryl thought, *we're getting somewhere*.

When Phoebe returned to Halliwell Manor, it was quiet.

That was unexpected. The house was almost never utterly silent, and she had fully expected Piper to be blaring her Meg Winship video in the living room. "Piper?" she called. "Paige?"

There was no answer.

"Leo?"

This time, at least, there was a response. Leo orbed into the room and stood beside her. "Where's Piper?" he inquired.

"That's what I was going to ask you."

"I don't know," he said. "I've been at the club, supervising the plumbers because Piper was so wrapped up in her workout. I thought she was still here."

"She was when I left," Phoebe said.

"What about Paige?"

"She was going to go back to see her old professor again," Phoebe told him. "To try to get some more concrete information out of him."

Leo looked a little nervous, Phoebe thought. "Do you sense that Piper's in any danger?" she asked.

"No. Wherever she is, she feels safe," he insisted. "But that doesn't mean she *is* safe. We thought she was okay after the ritual last night, but then today she was back at it. Since she hasn't been acting like herself lately, we can't take anything for granted."

Phoebe nodded, but wasn't sure she totally agreed. Yes, his wife was missing. But that might have been a good thing—it might mean that she'd overcome this fixation with the exercise video and gone shopping or something. "I'll call her cell. Maybe she went to the club and you guys missed each other when you orbed."

"Or I could orb back and see," Leo suggested. He crossed to the window, anxiously looking for his wife.

"The club was just a suggestion, Leo. She could have gone shopping, or—"

Leo cut her off. "Her car's still here," he pointed out. "Wherever she went, she went on foot."

"So maybe she just wanted some air," Phoebe countered, getting a little nervous herself now. She crossed to a phone and dialed the number of Piper's cell. It rang several times, but there was no answer. She reported as much to Leo.

"Try Paige," he said.

While she was dialing, though, the front door opened.

"Piper?" Leo called.

"Paige," Paige replied. "Where's Piper?"

"Piper's not here," Phoebe explained. "We were hoping maybe you knew where she was."

"No clue," Paige said. She came into the living room, and Phoebe was surprised by her breathless expression. Her cheeks were rosy— okay, Phoebe thought, rosier than usual—with excitement. "But you guys, listen. Dr. Haywood was murdered, while I was at his house."

"Murdered?" Phoebe echoed, shocked at this turn of events. "Are you okay?"

"I'm fine," Paige assured her. "I was inside, he was outside."

Phoebe regarded her sister closely, and she did look okay. Phoebe was concerned—first Piper had gone workout-crazy, and now Paige was mixed up in a murder. The Charmed Ones faced all kinds of dangers, all the time, and Phoebe knew Paige could take care of herself. But still . . . things seemed to be spiraling toward trouble. And when that happened, there was usually a demon behind it. But there was no hint of a demon at this point. Phoebe's mind tried to connect any dots she could imagine. What if the murder was somehow related to whatever was going on with Piper? Sure, it was a stretch—but stranger things had happened.

Now she was just as anxious as Leo had been. Paige described her afternoon—the visit with Dr. Haywood, the murder—and the fact that the only people she had seen in the neighborhood were a couple of apparently innocent joggers.

"Joggers?" she repeated when Paige described them. "Were they listening to workout tapes?"

"I don't know," Paige said. "Maybe."

"Phoebe, the Bay Area is a pretty health-conscious region," Leo reminded her. "You can't automatically be suspicious of anyone who works out in any way."

"I'm not," Phoebe objected. "I'm just . . . looking for connections. Common threads. Just in case. Isn't that what the police do when a murder is committed?"

Leo was peering out the window again, but he turned around and crossed his arms over his chest. "I guess," he said. "But I'd know if anything had happened to Piper."

"But Piper's definitely got something going on, Leo. It may be jamming your Whitelighter radar," Phoebe offered. "And Paige was on the scene of a murder. I know there's no definite link, but that doesn't mean I'm not a little freaked out."

"Well, I am too," Leo admitted. "Especially with Piper not answering her phone, and leaving her car here." He pressed his lips together in a thin line, and a frown wrinkled his brow. "Whether she thinks she needs us or not, I think we need to do something."

"Okay, so where do we go from here?" Paige asked.

"Backward," Phoebe replied.

Paige gave her a quizzical look.

"The last time we saw her she was watching that stupid tape," Phoebe declared. "I think we need to pay a visit to Meg Winship."

Chapter
9

"Palatial" was one word to describe Meg Winship's estate. As a journalist, Bill Conason made a mental note in case he had the opportunity to describe the estate in a story. Since meeting with Phoebe, he'd been snooping around the UFO story. He didn't know what she knew, and she obviously wasn't talking. But he now believed there was more to it, he had become convinced, and somehow it all tied back to Meg Winship.

Job stability was very important to him. Earlier in his career, it hadn't mattered so much. He'd worked in TV, in radio, and at newspapers in big markets and small. He'd moved around when he had to—Philadelphia, Des Moines, Saint Petersburg, Houston, finally San Francisco. There had been a kind of excitement, almost a romance, to it all. The nomadic newsman, going wherever there was a gig or a story.

Eventually, he'd begun to realize that he wasn't exactly leaving friends in his wake. He was either fired from every job, or he had quit. Every gig he'd left behind had narrowed his possibilities for future employment. As other people in the business moved around, too, his reputation spread even to places he had never been. Recently, he'd sent out a couple of feelers, just in case things soured here in San Francisco, and he'd been turned down flat.

He had been broke before, in the earliest days of his career. He hadn't liked it one bit. But that had been a lot of years ago. Now, he was older. He had credit card bills to pay, and his rent was a lot more than the third-floor walkup he'd had then, and he was on the hook for some gambling debts he should have known better than to get behind on. Bill wasn't a guy who could afford to lose his job, but he was a guy who kept an ear close to the ground, and he knew that job security in the newspaper business was as bad as it had ever been.

Making a real story out of tabloid fodder like a UFO invasion would be hard work. But this was the kind of story that would cancel out a lot of bad rumors, a lot of bland reporting. It's a star-making story, he was convinced. And he wanted it as badly as he'd ever wanted anything in his life.

He had parked across the street from the gate to Winship's world. It was on a lane that felt rural, even though Sausalito was just five minutes away. The gate was shaded by a giant willow tree that must have been a hundred years old; behind the ten-foot stucco wall he could see towering redwoods. From the gate, which wasn't guarded but had an electronic call box, a winding gravel drive led up a grassy hill. The drive disappeared now and again in shallow valleys, but it didn't matter—its ultimate destination was easily seen, commanding the top of the hill. Meg Winship's house looked like something the old kings of France might have lived in, on the banks of the Loire. The walls were pale yellow, the color of morning sunlight. The mansard roof gleamed, a patchwork of multicolored slates. Its windows were large and arched; Bill was sure that Meg could see the bay, and probably San Francisco itself, from them. A million-dollar view, that was for sure.

From his own apartment Bill could see the wall of the building across the alley, brick that had been painted white once but then was never painted again, stained with grease from the Chinese restaurant downstairs, worn by wind and weather. Not that he resented Meg Winship's millions—she had earned it, he figured, and if he could have come up with a gimmick that sold like hers did, he'd be right there on the hilltop next to her.

But he had a newsman's suspicious nature, so he figured that anyone who had made such fast money probably had buried some skeletons somewhere along the way. He wasn't ready to confront her yet—he wanted to do some more digging before he did that. But he'd wanted this glimpse of her natural habitat before he really began turning over rocks. He wanted to know who he'd be dealing with. Seeing her home—her palace—told him all he felt he needed to know.

Meg Winship was filthy rich. She lived like the villain in a James Bond movie. And all over the city, people who had apparently been abducted by flying saucers were turning to her workout videos like she was some kind of messiah.

Bill was no James Bond, but if he'd absorbed nothing else in journalism school, he had learned that journalists have a responsibility to stand up to the powerful. He would do that now. Meg Winship's wealth had made her powerful; the connection to the UFOs made her a story.

The only thing Bill had to worry about now was Phoebe Halliwell getting to it first. He took one last look at the gate and the big walls, and then put his car into gear and drove away.

Paige and Phoebe stepped up to the front gate. It was wide enough for two cars to pass each other going through—maybe two city buses, for that matter—and it looked like the kind of gate that should be guarded by armed men. *Probably vicious dogs on the other side, too*, Paige thought. But there was no one in sight.

"Here's an intercom," Phoebe pointed out. Paige reached past her and pushed the button. Almost immediately, a voice responded, electronics removing all character and even disguising the speaker's gender.

"May I help you?"

"Yes," Phoebe said. "We'd . . . um . . . like to see Meg Winship."

"I'm sorry, Ms. Winship is not accepting visitors."

Phoebe and Paige locked eyes. Then Paige leaned closer to the box. "Look, this is Phoebe Halliwell from the *Bay Mirror,* and if we can't see Meg Winship, there's going to be trouble."

"Paige!" Phoebe said sharply. "What trouble?"

"Okay, not trouble," Paige said toward the intercom box. "But I could potentially embarrass Ms. Winship in the paper. Or . . . or if Ms. Winship ever has a personal problem and needs advice, I wouldn't give it."

"One moment, please," the voice said.

"See?" Paige said. "You have to get tough with people sometime. Throw your weight around."

The box clicked once, indicating that the connection had been broken.

"Maybe I don't have as much weight to throw as you'd like to think," Phoebe lamented.

They were not going to take that as a brush-off, though. They were prepared to camp out in Meg Winship's driveway until she sicced the dogs on them, or came out herself. She had to leave the house eventually.

Static came from the electronic box, surprising them. Then the voice returned. "Ms. Winship can spare five minutes. Do you have a car?"

Paige looked toward where they'd parked it, on the shoulder of the country lane. "Yeah, we'll get it. Just give us two minutes."

"Very well," the voice said, and then cut off again. With a buzzing sound, the gate began to open.

Paige had waited in many places in her life, but not many as luxurious as this one. Still, fancy wallpaper, beautiful Italian tile floor, and antique French furniture aside, waiting was waiting, and at a certain point it was just downright rude. Besides which, while the furniture was lovely, the chair she'd been shown to was hard and rigid and absolutely straight, made only for people composed of strict right angles instead of soft curves. There was no way to get comfortable in it.

After trying for a while, she gave up and stood, wandering over to a bookshelf. She and Phoebe had been left in some kind of den, decorated with an antique desk that seemed never to have been used, a couch, a couple of chairs, one of those huge old globes that showed what the world would look like if it were all sepia tones, and some bookshelves. There weren't actually many books on the shelves, though. Of the ones that were there, most were multiple copies of Meg Winship's own titles. *The Winship Workout, The Winship Way,* and *Your Ideal You,* in hardcover and paperback editions. On the walls, in ornate gold frames, were photographs of Meg Winship, including ones from the covers of the books and others from their interior pages: Meg in skimpy workout wear that emphasized the firmness of her stomach, the musculature of her arms and shoulders, the power of her calves and thighs.

"This woman is kind of pleased with herself, isn't she?" Paige asked quietly.

"Wouldn't you be?" Phoebe replied. "She looks great."

"Yeah, well, we look pretty good, too, and yet we don't decorate our home exclusively with photos of us."

Since being brought to the den by a female employee in a traditional business suit, they hadn't seen a living soul. Bored and more than a little annoyed, Paige went into the hallway. The décor here was similar to that in the den, except the walls were lined with massive oil paintings, and Meg Winship was not the subject of any of them. They looked like originals, and though Paige didn't know that much about Renaissance art, she was pretty sure they were the real deal.

From a room farther down the hall, she heard feminine voices in hushed conversation. Boredom stirred curiosity. Walking as quietly as she could manage in her pointy kitten heels, Paige eased toward the open doorway and peeked inside.

Seven women were standing at long tables, working on a kind of assembly line. The one on the near end would open a colorful paper folder and put one item in it, then pass it on to the next woman. Each woman would add something else from stacks in front of her—photos of Meg Winship, press releases, a photocopied interview. The last woman in line was taking the folders and arranging them neatly in large cardboard boxes.

Paige hadn't really noticed any of the women, beyond their appointed tasks, until the folder stacker made a familiar flip of her ponytail.

It was Piper!

Paige hurried back down the hall, again trying to be quiet. "Phoebe!" she stage-whispered from the doorway to the den. Her sister was standing restlessly at a front window. "Piper's here!"

Phoebe spun around quickly. "She's here? Where?"

"Down the hall," Paige answered. "Working. Stuffing bags."

Phoebe crossed the big den, and together they went back to the other room, this time not worrying about making noise. Instead of peeking, they just walked into the workroom. "Piper," Phoebe said firmly. "What are you doing here?"

Piper put a bag into the big box and then turned to face them. "Hi, Phoebes. Hi, Paige."

"Piper," Paige said. "You didn't answer her question."

Piper looked at them both with a half-smile on her face, as if the question had been too silly to warrant an answer. "Working," she said. "Guys, these are my sisters, Phoebe and Paige."

"Hi, Phoebe and Paige," the other women said, almost in unison. Though they varied in age and body type, they were all dressed in workout clothes.

"Working on what?" Phoebe demanded.

"We're stuffing bags," Piper said casually. "For attendees of Meg's rally and seminar tomorrow."

"Hundreds will be there," one of the women said.

"We're stuffing a thousand bags," another announced. "But I don't think that'll be enough."

"Meg is so wonderful," a fourth said. "It's going to be such an exciting day."

"Yeah," Phoebe said, not sounding convinced. "Piper, we need to talk to you."

"Okay," Piper said, bending over to put the next bag away.

"Alone," Phoebe clarified. "Not here."

"Oh, I'm sorry, Phoebe. I'm much too busy for that. A thousand bags is a lot of bags. And we might need more." *Piper's voice is unnaturally cheerful,* Paige thought. *Has she been brainwashed, somehow? Is that what this is all about?*

"So I've heard," Phoebe said. "But what about the club? The plumbing problems?"

"Leo can take care of that. Right now, this is my top priority. And if you really need to talk, we can talk on Sunday," Piper continued. "After the rally."

"Umm, Sunday might be too late," Paige put in. "Today would be better."

"She said Sunday," one of the other women snapped. They all turned to glare at Phoebe and Paige.

"Sorry, but she's our sister," Phoebe insisted. "Piper, now."

"We're all sisters," Piper replied. The smile hadn't left her face, even though the other women all looked like they were ready for a fight. "Sisters in our empowerment."

Phoebe gave Piper an ingratiating smile. "Can we talk in private for a second?" she asked. "Maybe in another room?"

Paige understood immediately. To orb Piper out of here, they had to get her away from these other women, someplace where they wouldn't be observed. Piper shrugged, glancing at her co-workers. Some of the other women scowled, as if they didn't like the idea, but no one moved to stop her.

As soon as they were all out in the empty hallway, Phoebe grabbed Piper's hand, and Paige's. "Orb us out of here," she whispered.

"Got it," Paige returned with a nod. She

orbed back to the car, parked in the big circular driveway in front of the house. But when they arrived, she and Phoebe were alone.

"Where's Piper?" Phoebe asked.

"I don't know," Paige said.

"She must have let go of my hand! Go back."

Paige tried to comply, but immediately felt a sensation that she guessed was not unlike ramming her head at full speed into a large, flat rock. She staggered and fell down on the pavement.

Phoebe was looking at her querulously.

"What?" Paige demanded. "I'll do it, just hold on." She tried again to orb back into the house, but was thrown back again. "Ow!" she complained.

"What's the matter?"

Paige rubbed her forehead. "Does this look flat to you?"

"Paige, what's going on? Why aren't you inside?"

"I don't know!" Paige grumped. "I can't orb back in. It's like there's some kind of force field."

"You have to get Piper!" Phoebe reminded her.

Duh, I didn't hit my head that *hard,* Paige thought. "I know that. I'm trying, I just can't get through."

"There must be magic protecting the house," Phoebe said. But how? Was Meg Winship a witch? Is that how she was controlling these women?

"I think so," Paige said. It bothered her that she could orb out but not back in. She hated to be frustrated at anything, but especially at witchcraft, at which—although she'd had a late start—she believed she had become pretty good.

"I guess there's only one alternative," Phoebe said.

"What is it?"

Phoebe nodded toward the front door. "We knock."

Paige agreed. "Oh, yeah. That'll work."

In fact, the door opened before they'd even had a chance to touch it. This time, though, they weren't met by a single, business suit–clad woman, but by four tall, muscular women dressed in pink sports bras, jogging shorts, and sneakers. Looking at their powerful physiques— broad shoulders, massive upper arms, corded thighs—Paige felt very small.

Phoebe could take them, Paige thought. Between her martial arts skills and her levitation powers, even four Amazons didn't stand a chance. And these weren't real Amazons anyway, just figurative Amazons. She noticed that Phoebe had tensed, and believed her sister was probably weighing the odds as well. The women were smiling at them, but the mood had changed. Confrontation was in the air.

"Ms. Winship is ready to see you now," one of them announced.

Chapter
10

Darryl could have spent the rest of the year searching Carter Haywood's house without finding anything useful. Instead, he assigned that task to a couple of uniformed officers and took a trip across the bay, to Berkeley, one of the few places around where hippies were not an endangered species. A few minutes in the administrative office of U.C. Berkeley pointed him toward Dr. Mark Arendt, who had once shared an office with Haywood. Arendt looked like a hippie himself, one who had kept the long hair and beard, anyway, although he wore a red, patterned tie with his blue chambray work shirt and corduroy pants. *Working-class hero*, thought Darryl. *Probably popular with the coeds.*

"Help you?" he asked when Darryl entered the office. "You're not a student."

"No, I'm not," Darryl said. He guessed that

Arendt had been glad to lose his slob of an officemate—his space was immaculate, books neatly arranged on shelves, papers tucked away in filing cabinets. On his desk was an open laptop computer, a telephone, a coffee mug containing pens and pencils, and nothing else. "Actually, I'm a police detective from San Francisco."

"Little outside your jurisdiction here," the professor commented.

"That's right," Darryl admitted. "I'm just here looking for some information about Dr. Carter Haywood. I understand you used to share an office with him."

Arendt nodded. "Yes. A few years back. He got mixed up in an unfortunate situation, and I ended up with a private office. Silver lining, right?"

Darryl indicated an empty guest chair. "Mind if I sit?"

"Knock yourself out," Arendt offered. "Don't know how much help I can be, though. I haven't talked to Carter since he left the school."

"You're not going to, then," Darryl said. "He was murdered earlier today."

Arendt's face fell, the frown accentuating his age. He was much younger than Haywood, but still in his fifties, Darryl guessed. There was as much gray as brown in his beard and ponytail. "I'm really sorry to hear that. You know who did it?"

"Still working on that," Darryl admitted. "I

was hoping you could tell me a little more about why he left the school, what exactly happened back then."

Arendt settled back in his old wooden desk chair. "I guess it's okay to talk about it now," he said. "Considering it's not likely to upset Carter any."

"Was he secretive about it?" Darryl asked. If he had been, then that might have been a source of conflict—in the course of trying to protect his secret, he'd made some enemy who'd ended up killing him.

Arendt shook his head slowly. "I guess his whole problem was that he wasn't secretive enough," he said. "I never liked to blab about him, you know. But he didn't have sense enough to keep quiet when he should have."

"About what?" Darryl prodded. He knew what Paige had told him, but her details had been sparse.

The professor steepled his hands on his desk and rested his forehead on his fingertips. "I don't know how much you know," he began, "but Carter was pretty seriously into flying saucers, extraterrestrials, all that stuff."

"I've heard that," Darryl said.

"Yeah, he didn't try to hide it. It was bad enough when he used to talk about it in class—going on about aliens among us, mysterious abductions, you know—but what finally finished his career were the experiments he conducted.

Borrowing equipment from astronomy, physics, and photography departments. He absolutely believed that there were flying saucers around, and that the only reason they weren't better known was that people refused to believe in them. When he had concrete evidence, they'd all come over to his point of view."

"So what happened?"

Arendt smiled. "As always, he couldn't keep his mouth shut. The administration wanted to look the other way, but when he involved a student in the experiments, they couldn't ignore him anymore. Pulling crazy stunts yourself is one thing, but enlisting student help is beyond acceptable, I guess."

"And so he got fired," Darryl guessed.

"That's right. I guess the administration was worried about parents freaking out, pulling their kids, demanding tuition refunds."

"All of which would be frowned upon."

"You got it. When you put the tuition money in danger, action gets taken. Carter was out before he could turn around."

"Did he have any enemies that you know of?" Darryl asked. "Perhaps his ideas personally upset someone?"

"Not anyone who'd be ticked off enough to kill him," Arendt said. "People mostly liked him—or, at least, you know, tolerated him. He was the archetypal absentminded professor. Very, very good in his specialties. He just allowed himself to get carried away by these theories of his—crackpot theories, to put it mildly—to the point that they ruined his life."

"And maybe ended it," Darryl added.

"I suppose," Arendt said. "He published a little after he left here, but just lunatic fringe stuff, you know? No one in the academic community took him seriously anymore."

"One more thing," Darryl said, "and then I'll get out of your hair. Do you remember a student of his named Meg Winship?"

Mark Arendt straightened up, his face brightening. "Of course," he said. "I mean, even if she hadn't become famous, I'd remember her. Guess I didn't mention it, but the student who got involved in Carter's experiments? That was Meg. When he got fired, she took it hard. Quit her T.A. job; changed her major. I think that's when she started in on the fitness kick, exchanging physical achievement for academic. She dropped out; never graduated. But hey, who can argue it didn't pay off for her? She must make more in a year than any dozen philosophers in their whole lifetimes."

"You're probably right," Darryl said. He had known that Meg and Carter Haywood were acquaintances. But the fact that Meg had worked with him in his UFO research put a different spin on things, cementing the connection—although he still couldn't figure out quite how—between the current rash of abductions and the strange Meg Winship mania that gripped the city. "Did you know her very well?" he asked.

"She was around a lot, I guess. And Carter talked about her plenty."

"What do you remember?"

Arendt tugged at his beard for a moment. "Scholarship student," he said. "Dirt poor, I think. Her parents died when she was very young, Carter said, and she was raised in a succession of foster homes. I don't remember any particularly awful stories about them, but she was left essentially penniless. When she got into school, she didn't know anybody, and I can't recall her ever bringing any friends around when she came to see Carter. I think she was a loner, kind of sad, and she latched on to Carter as if he were her salvation. There was one morning that he was sick and didn't make it to campus, and she sat around the office for hours, like she just didn't have anyplace else to go."

He fell silent. "Is that it?" Darryl pressed.

"All I can remember in any detail," Arendt answered. "I just have an impression of a kind of mopey girl. I felt sorry for her. Anyone who would hero-worship Carter like that, I thought, must have a pretty empty life." He smiled. "Not anymore, huh? I guess she's got everything she needs now."

"You're the philosophy professor," Darryl observed. "Does anyone ever have everything she needs? Or believe that she does?"

Arendt jabbed a finger at the detective. "Point to you," he said. "You ever want to hang up the badge, maybe you've got a career here."

Darryl smiled. "I don't think so." He thanked Arendt and walked out onto the campus, crowded as late afternoon classes let out. Somehow, he had to figure out what bond still held Winship and Haywood years after he had ceased to be her teacher. And he definitely had to call the Halliwells and let them know about this twist. Taking his cell phone from an inside pocket of his blazer, he dialed their home.

No one answered. He left a brief message, then closed the phone, determined to try again later.

"I understand that you've seen Piper," Meg Winship said. Phoebe and Paige had been led back to the den, where Meg had taken a seat behind the desk. Phoebe, still steaming, had chosen to stand, but Paige sat down again in the chair she'd had when they were first put in here to wait. The four enormous women had left them alone after everyone was situated.

"That's right," Phoebe said, unconsciously clenching her fists. "And we plan to take her with us when we go."

Meg smiled the thousand-megawatt smile that graced her book and video covers. Her blond hair was short and neatly coiffed, her tan pants and jacket outfit casually expensive.

Understated gold jewelry adorned her wrists, neck, and ears. She was a little younger than Paige, but she had the self-confidence and poise of a successful woman decades older, the kind who could run a corporate empire. "But, why?" Meg asked. "As you've seen, Piper's perfectly well and happy here. She's doing valuable work, helping to prepare for my seminar tomorrow. In a very short time she's become an extremely valued asset."

"So she's working for you?" Paige demanded. "Is that what you're trying to tell us?"

"On a strictly volunteer basis," Meg answered. "I have very little paid staff. Luckily, there are so many women who have found their lives improved by my work and want to do whatever they can to give something back."

"I'll bet," Paige grumped.

Meg looked both Halliwells up and down. "You're both in very good shape," she said. "Have you tried my program?"

"No," Phoebe said. "*So* not interested."

Meg glanced toward the ceiling, then back at them, as if trying to get a handle on some sudden anger. "I have to confess, I really don't understand your antagonism. Your sister, as I pointed out, is perfectly fine. She's free to leave anytime she chooses. I do appreciate her help, and would love for her to stay on until after the seminar, but it's entirely up to her."

"Then we'll all be going now," Paige said.

"Note, I said 'up to her.'" Meg reminded them. "She's an adult, perfectly in control of her own faculties, correct?"

"Yes, of course," Paige answered.

"If you were to try to remove her against her will, that would be kidnapping," Meg pointed out.

"Excuse me, but she's our sister!" Phoebe snapped.

"Indeed. And, as mentioned, an adult. She can make her own decisions."

"And if she's being held here against her will, isn't that kidnapping too?" Phoebe asked.

"You're free to ask her," Meg parried. She pushed a button on her phone, and a voice answered immediately.

"Yes, Ms. Winship?"

"Please ask Piper to come in," Meg said.

"Right away," the voice replied.

Phoebe was convinced that there was some kind of brainwashing going on—that somehow, Meg's videos carried a subliminal suggestion or something that had entrapped her sister, as well as thousands of other local women. And somehow, it tied in to the UFO abductions that had been occurring, although how? Piper had never been "abducted." Meg looked perfectly human, not alien in the least, and Phoebe couldn't figure out how the two matched up.

Phoebe's mind was whirling, trying to figure out how Meg could have magically blocked the house—and, more importantly, why. And what was she? A demon? Could there really be aliens, and did they have some sort of magical powers? That was really not an option, as far as Phoebe was concerned, but it angered her to know that they couldn't simply enter and take Piper out at any time. But the fact was, they were here now, and they weren't leaving without their sister.

The same four women who had answered the door escorted Piper in. Piper looked just as she had in the workroom: perfectly happy and relaxed.

"Okay," Phoebe whispered to Paige. "Orb us all out of here."

She saw Paige tense, and then shake a little in her chair. "I can't," Paige said. "Still blocked."

Phoebe decided to try a different tactic. She turned back to Piper. "Come on, sis. We've got to take you home now. Leo is worried sick about you."

"He'll be fine," Piper said, the smile still plastered to her face. "He's a big boy."

"Yeah, big and tough," Paige pointed out. "If he finds out you wouldn't come home, he'll be here in a flash, and he won't be happy."

"Are you satisfied?" Meg asked them. "Piper, do you want to leave with them, or not?"

"I still have too much to do," Piper answered. "We have to finish getting ready for tomorrow."

"And after tomorrow," Meg pressed. "Then will you go home to Leo?"

"Of course," Piper said casually. "He's my husband, right?"

Meg looked at Phoebe and Paige with a self-satisfied smirk on her pretty face. "Well, ladies?"

Phoebe noted that the four strong women had remained in the room. They could try to just take Piper by force. It would be a hard, physical fight, and people might get hurt.

Well, whatever, she thought. *You'll just have to make sure the ones getting hurt are the ones on the other side.*

But Phoebe didn't really want to start a brawl. Brains first, brawn as a last resort. Especially since they were outclassed in the brawn department. She walked over to Piper, stopping directly in front of her big sister. The women— Meg's Musclewomen, she was coming to think of them—tensed. They were ready for her to start something. But she just touched Piper's arm and looked into her eyes. "Are you sure, Piper? This is *that* important to you?"

"Phoebes," Piper said, and she sounded like . . . like Piper. Not like a zombie, not like a prisoner. "I'm fine, really. I just want to help out here. I think it's important. You can get that, can't you? This is something I want to do. I need to do. Okay?"

"Yeah," Phoebe said, surprised and taken a little off-balance by Piper's apparent sincerity. She hadn't expected that. There had been times that Piper had been possessed by other spirits, or enchanted in such a way that her decisions weren't entirely her own. Phoebe couldn't shake the feeling that the same thing had happened here. But generally when that happened, Piper came across un-Piper-like. Not this time. Piper *was* Piper—looked like Piper, sounded like Piper—she had just made a decision that Phoebe and Paige didn't agree with. "Yeah, okay."

"What do you mean, okay?" Paige wanted to know. "*Not* okay. Not okay at all."

"Paige," Phoebe said, "I think we have to let her do this." She wondered for a moment if she had become enchanted, too, if those words were really escaping her lips.

"What," Paige demanded, "just let her stay here with these . . . these . . ." But she was unable to finish her sentence. Phoebe understood. The women surrounding them were powerful, imposing, but they just looked like women. Meg Winship was strong and successful, but she was also . . . well, nice. No one had treated them with anything but civility since they'd come to this house.

But their witchcraft didn't work here, except one way: out. That was extremely worrying. Still, Piper was fine, physically, and didn't seem to be in any real danger. "Yeah," Phoebe said. "Yeah, I think we can leave her here."

Paige started to object, but then just closed her mouth.

"You're positive, Piper?" Phoebe asked.

"Of course," Piper answered quickly. "Tell Leo I'm fine and I'll see him tomorrow night, okay?"

"Okay," Phoebe agreed. She still wasn't altogether comfortable with her own decision. But starting a brawl in order to take Piper away from someplace she clearly wanted to be was no better. "But if you don't come home tomorrow night after the rally or whatever it is, we'll be back." She directed her closing statement toward Meg. "And we'll be angry."

Piper gave Phoebe a quick hug, and even her body language made Phoebe think they'd made the right choice. She didn't feel especially tense or upset in any way. "Let's get out of here, Paige," Phoebe suggested.

"Yeah, okay," Paige said. She still seemed kind of shell-shocked by the whole thing.

"Come again anytime," Meg Winship offered.

One of Meg's Musclewomen led them back to the front door. Paige didn't say another word until they were in the car, with the motor running. "Are you crazy?" she asked, anger evident in her tone. "We can't just drive away and leave Piper in there!"

"Sure we can," Phoebe countered. "We're doing it. It's the only thing we can do."

"And then what? Just hope she really does come home tomorrow?"

"Of course not," Phoebe told her. "Then we get Leo and we come back. It'd take the Power of Three to break through whatever magical defenses surround this place, and we don't have that without Piper. But with Leo on our side, we're still a force to be reckoned with."

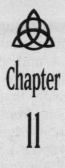

Chapter

11

Meg laughed to herself.

She had effectively neutralized the Charmed Ones— prevented them from using the Power of Three against her. Countless demons had tried, and failed, but she—a human, at that!—had managed it. Not without help, she knew, and guidance. But still, it had been her own idea, and it had worked.

As the rest of her plan would.

She had spent months, after Dr. Haywood's fall from academic grace, studying and learning and exploring. She had taken his theories in directions he was afraid to pursue. She had made connections that he had missed entirely, intuitive leaps he'd been unable to manage. The student had far surpassed the teacher.

The more she learned, the more she needed to know. Ultimately, she reached a point where it all unfolded for her, though, and she understood. She was able to draw back the veil between dimensions, and she made the contact she had been seeking.

And having made that contact, she had opened the most important door—the one to absolute power. Knowledge alone wasn't good enough. Dr. Haywood's knowledge had been impressive, but still, the university officials had broken him because they'd had power and he hadn't. Money wasn't enough either. There were plenty of rich people, even successful, well-known people who couldn't, for all their wealth and prestige, control what the future would bring. Wealthier people than Meg had been wiped out because they didn't know what tomorrow held.

That would not happen to her. She would not only know, she would dictate tomorrow. And the next day, and the one after that.

Dr. Haywood had set her on the right path, after all. He hadn't known it—would never know it, as it turned out, since he hadn't lived to see it all come to fruition. But he'd been the first one to glimpse the light, and for that, Meg would always be grateful.

Even with Leo's assistance, Phoebe and Paige couldn't orb back into Meg Winship's compound. Some powerful force kept them at bay—the closest they could get was the street on the outside of the gate. Paige was about to go back to the intercom and buzz to get back in when Leo stopped her. "Don't bother," he said.

"What?" She was positive that she had misheard him. He was the most concerned, caring husband she had ever heard of. There was no way he'd rest while Piper was inside that place.

"You said she seemed fine, right?" he asked Phoebe.

"I've known Piper my whole life, and she was fine," Phoebe said adamantly. "She was Piper. I can't explain it, but she didn't seem like a prisoner in any way. She just wanted to stay."

"Then I guess we let her do it," Leo said.

Paige looked at Leo like he was the one now possessed. "This is a joke, right?"

"No, Paige. Piper's been acting . . . a little strange, lately. Something's been bothering her, and she hasn't been willing to tell me what. Or else she couldn't figure it out herself. But if this is really something she wants, something that'll help her—"

"But Leo," Paige broke in, "they're *holding* her there somehow."

"Maybe they are," Leo admitted. He looked glum, but resigned. "But maybe she's doing it. Maybe it's what *she* wants. If she wouldn't leave with you when she had a chance, I think we have to respect that."

"I agree," Phoebe said. "This is what she wants."

"Anyway," Leo added, "I don't see that we have much of a choice. If Piper really does want this, I don't want to storm in there and try to take her away. It sounds like she's fine, and not in any danger. The rally's tomorrow. If she doesn't come home after that, then we'll come back and throw everything we've got at the place."

Paige still thought they were both giving up too easily. But she couldn't disagree with Phoebe's assessment of Piper's behavior: Piper *had* seemed perfectly normal, perfectly rational, and capable of making her own decisions.

Still, Paige didn't trust Meg Winship for a second. And how many moguls—even well-known ones with familiar faces, like Meg—had their own mystical shields? She was pretty sure that not even an Oprah Winfrey or a Bill Gates had something like that.

"Okay," she relented. "If you guys are sure. . . ."

"One night, Paige," Phoebe promised. "That's all. Tomorrow, she comes home or we come back and take the place down brick by brick, force field or no."

"That's right," Leo confirmed. "Let's go home now, so we can work on figuring out what's really going on here."

Paige shrugged, not happy about being outvoted but willing to go along with the majority— for the moment. She orbed them home.

When they reached Halliwell Manor, the phone was ringing. Paige was closest, and she grabbed it. "Hello?"

"Hi, Paige," a familiar voice said. "It's Darryl Morris. I left you a message." Paige had been so wrapped up in worrying about Piper that she had almost forgotten her old professor had been murdered. "Hi, Darryl," she said. "Have you found out who killed Dr. Haywood?"

"Unfortunately, no," Darryl replied. "But I did find something I think you ought to know about." He described the book he'd found, inscribed to Dr. Haywood by Meg Winship, and then told her about his visit with Dr. Haywood's former office mate. "It doesn't mean she had anything to do with his death," he pointed out when he was finished. "But it proves that there's some connection between them—or there was. I'm trying to get copies of his phone records now, to see if they were in contact recently."

"Okay, Darryl," Paige said, trying to process everything he'd told her. "Thanks for the update. Let me know if you find out anything else."

"You do the same," he replied.

"Of course," she said, knowing that if she did, she'd have to tell him about seeing Piper at Meg's home. Unless Meg became directly linked to Dr. Haywood's death, she didn't want to get Piper any more involved.

After hanging up, Paige told Phoebe and Leo

what Darryl had said. Both shared her concern, but it didn't seem to change their minds about going back for Piper. "That doesn't mean Meg murdered anyone. And we don't know what she wants Piper for," Leo pointed out. "But as long as she does, Piper should be safe there."

"What happens if she doesn't need Piper alive anymore?" Paige wondered.

"Piper can take care of herself," Phoebe reminded her. "And it's only one night."

Paige wasn't crazy about the "only one night" mantra Phoebe and Leo had adopted. But they still outnumbered her, and there was nothing she could do on her own—she'd already found *that* out the hard way. Paige went upstairs to see if she could learn any more from Dr. Haywood's book.

"Do you know Meg Winship? I mean, personally?"

Henry Ralston, the store manager, shifted on his stool. He was a healthy-looking guy, with muscular arms that strained the sleeves of his blue polo shirt, a deep chest, and a narrow waist. Bill Conason sat facing him, legs crossed, with his little notebook on his knee and a pen in hand. They were behind the checkout counter of Play Ball, one of the city's big independent sporting goods stores, and Henry wanted to stay on the floor because he was short-handed that day. Bill had wanted to interview him alone in his office, where he might be more forthcoming, but it clearly wasn't going to work out that way.

"Well, you know, I've met her. She did a signing here when her last book came out."

"That would be *Your Ideal You*," Bill prodded.

"That's right. It was very successful, more than two hundred people came out to meet her"

"Good crowd. So she's been pretty popular for a while now."

"Oh, sure," Henry replied. "Steady seller in books, videos, and workout clothing and accessories. She's a brand name, and it's a good one. People associate Meg Winship with high quality and a healthy lifestyle."

"Good things in a fitness expert," Bill said.

"Yeah."

"But in the past few weeks, would you say that interest in her line has increased?"

"Oh, yeah," Henry said again. "Yeah, definitely. There's been a boom in the Winship lines. Hard to keep her in stock."

"What do you attribute that to?" Bill asked. "Anything in particular?"

"Excuse me." Henry looked toward the cash register, where a woman in a pink satin warm-up jacket was perusing the maps and guidebooks displayed on the counter. "Can I help you?" he asked her.

She tossed a quick smile his way. "I'm just looking for now," she said.

Henry turned back to Bill. "I'm sorry, where were we?"

Bill watched the woman walk away from the counter and join a similarly attired friend, who was examining tennis gear. "I was asking if you have an opinion as to what's caused the Meg Winship boom you were talking about," he said.

"Right." Henry considered the question for a moment. "Well there's been an awful lot of publicity about her big event tomorrow," he said. "That might be driving some of it."

"What's that all about, anyway?" Bill asked.

"It's a kind of seminar," Henry said. "Getting a bunch of fans together, putting them through their paces—you know: work out with the master and get the benefit of her wisdom in person."

"So it's not just listening to her talk—she'll actually be leading them in some kind of mass fitness routine?"

"That's the impression I get. I know a lot of our customers are going to be there."

Bill glanced around the store again. There were a handful of people browsing, but no one had made a purchase since he'd sat down behind the counter.

"What do you think of Meg? On a personal level, I mean, not in terms of how much business she brings in."

"Not a prima donna at all," Henry said. "You know, some people with her kind of success would be standoffish, or make a lot of demands.

Not Meg. She was great to work with. I'd have her in the store anytime."

"So you haven't heard any strange rumors about her, anything kind of, you know, under-handed about the way she does business?"

"Oh, not at all," Henry replied immediately. "This is a small industry, really. If there had been any rumors like that, I'd have heard them, for sure."

Bill had interviewed enough people to know that he wasn't going to get any dirt from Henry Ralston, even if the guy did know something. "Listen, thanks for your help," he said, closing his notebook. He'd only jotted down a few random thoughts.

As he left, he noticed that the store seemed even emptier. Outside, the expansive parking lot was mostly vacant. Overhead lamps beamed down circles of light on the empty blacktop, illuminating the few vehicles that remained. As happened on most San Francisco nights, the day's warmth had quickly departed, and the air felt crisp and cool. His car was parked on the far side of the lot, away from the light that spilled from the store's big display windows.

He was almost to his SUV—more vehicle than he could reasonably afford, especially the way gas prices kept climbing—when a movement from between two other cars caught his eye. He started to turn his head, caught a momentary glimpse of pink coming toward him, and then he saw only bright flashes of light and realized the asphalt had somehow come up and scraped against his knees. Then he focused, realizing that he had fallen and that the flash of pink was the satin jacket of one of the women he'd seen inside. She stood just beyond his reach, panting with exertion.

But there had been two of them, he thought. *Where's the other?*

Before he had a chance to turn and look for her, something struck the back of his head, driving it forward. He caught himself on his palms, rubbing them raw on the rough surface of the lot, and tried to push himself upright. But more blows landed—kicks to his midsection—that doubled him over in pain. Bill Conason was reduced to squirming on the ground while the two assailants rained a savage attack down on him. He tried to cry out, but only a whimper would come. He found himself praying for blessed unconsciousness.

Even through eyes half-closed by swelling flesh and fogged with blood, he could see headlights sweeping the lot. His attackers saw them, too, and melted into the darkness. "You leave Meg alone," one of them said as she vanished, but through the roaring in his ears and the haze of pain, he wasn't sure he'd heard her right. He tried to rise, but couldn't, praying someone would spot him before he bled to death.

• • •

In the comfort of her own room, Paige went back to *The Visitors*, Dr. Haywood's book, convinced that there were answers in it—if only she knew where to look.

The words were just as meaningless as they'd been before, though. Dr. Haywood came off in the pages of his book like a crackpot, making intellectual leaps that just weren't supported by any evidence, ignoring facts that didn't fit his conclusions. He claimed that the lack of evidence backed his views—that if the aliens wanted to be well known, they could be, but that the limited and somewhat questionable nature of their sightings proved that they were successfully staying out of the limelight. This was, he opined, probably to better study Earth, without themselves changing the object of their research by becoming the center of attention.

It was the kind of argument that was hard to dispute, primarily because it was closed, not accepting any other interpretation of the available facts. Paige felt herself growing upset with her former teacher. He had somehow set himself up to be murdered, she thought, because he had clung to his ridiculous theories, and that had, in some way she didn't understand yet, angered someone enough to want him dead. And she'd been right there—she should have been able to stop it. That upset her all the more. If he had only cried out, he might still be alive. She could have run to his defense, and if she couldn't save him, maybe at least she would have some info that would help Darryl find the killer.

That's what was really getting to her, she reasoned. The Piper situation was bad enough. But if something happened to Piper because she wasn't there to protect her, that would be a million times worse than what had happened to Dr. Haywood. She knew her charge, as one of the Charmed Ones, was to protect Innocents, and she took that responsibility seriously. And she worried that Piper might somehow be her Innocent this time.

She tried to keep reading, to force herself to turn the pages, to not lose interest in spite of Dr. Haywood's bizarre theories. Finally, she needed to close her eyes for a few minutes, just to stop the words from spinning around inside her brain. But first she thumbed through the rest of the book just to see how much she still had to go.

Which was when she made a surprising discovery. Maybe Dr. Haywood hadn't chosen this particular copy of his book at random, after all. Penciled in the margins, near the back, were notes, which she could only assume were his. At first, they made no sense—a lot of equations, a few words by themselves, with no context. But as it got farther back in the book, there was more and more, written in a cramped, scratchy hand.

Alert again, Paige read through Dr. Haywood's notes, ignoring the book's text in favor of what had obviously been put down much more recently.

The more she read, the more she became filled with terror.

Finally, she searched the house, eventually finding Phoebe up in the attic, slumped over the Book of Shadows. She must have fallen asleep while paging through it looking for something on Meg or her crazy force field. "Phoebe, wake up!" she said urgently, shaking her sister's shoulder. "I have to show you something!"

Phoebe sat up suddenly, wrinkling the pages with her arms. "What is it?" she asked.

"This book," Paige said, waving it at her sister. "Dr. Haywood's book. I was reading it again, and I found this stuff in the back. These notes that he made."

"What notes?" Phoebe must have been deeply asleep, Paige thought, and was still having a hard time tracking.

"Dr. Haywood's notes," she said again. "In his book." She opened Dr. Haywood's book and pointed at his scattered handwriting. "He changed his mind about UFOs," she went on. "Just over the past year or so, I think, based on the dates he put down from time to time."

"What do you mean?" Phoebe asked, her eyes now focused. "What did he think they were?"

"Well, he used to be a pretty straightforward aliens guy," Paige said. "You know, UFOs were alien spaceships, sent here from other planets to study Earth."

"That makes sense, I guess," Phoebe said. "As much as anything else does, I mean."

"Yeah, but that was before," Paige pointed out. "Then he got a new idea. According to his notes, he was able to back it up with serious evidence. I don't know how . . . he's a little sketchy on that part. But he came to believe that they weren't from outer space at all."

"Where else could they be from?" Phoebe asked.

"He wasn't sure. But he thought they were from some other realm, some other plane of existence. In other words—"

"Demons? UFOs are demons?" Phoebe's eyes were wide open now, and a look of horror spread across her face.

"That's what he thought. I mean, he didn't say that specifically. But that's what it sounds like to me." Paige paused as Phoebe stood up and closed the Book. "It gets worse," she continued. "He had always thought the aliens were friendly. You know, scientifically curious, what with the probes and everything. But basically nice guys. Only now, he doesn't—well, didn't— think that. He became convinced that aliens were evil. And they sound like your garden-variety demon to me. Here, listen to this." She flipped through the book and began to read aloud. "'They seem determined to break down those walls and come here en masse, for their own sinister ends. To accomplish this, they will be relentless. Their scouts have learned much . . . our weaknesses and our strengths, and they will not suffer an easy defeat. It will be, I fear, a horrible time for all humanity. They will not stop . . .' And then it ends, as if he couldn't bring himself to write another word."

"Sounds like a few demons we've met," Phoebe said. "I'm amazed that Dr. Haywood figured it out, though."

"Apparently he met some of them, too. Or thought he did," Paige answered. "The question is, which demon was it, and is that who—or what—killed him?"

Chapter

12

Halliwell Manor felt strangely empty, even though everyone was home, except for Piper. Paige had never before realized just how much Piper contributed to the atmosphere of the big house. As the oldest sister, as the one the others looked up to for guidance and direction, Piper set the tone of the place, more than anyone else did. *It's not like we live in her shadow, or anything*, Paige thought. *Maybe more like she provides the sunlight that keeps us going.*

After Paige's revelation, Phoebe just stared at the book, silently willing it to give answers.

"Is there anything in there that tells you who killed your teacher?" Phoebe asked.

Paige shrugged and frowned. "Not precisely," she said. "It seems like he was afraid of something—afraid that what he was learning was putting him in some kind of danger. But from what, I can't tell exactly."

"From the UFOs themselves?" Phoebe pressed.

"Maybe," Paige replied. "If Dr. Haywood was right, then the UFOs are some kind of manifestation of demons from another plane of existence."

Leo entered, leaning on the doorjamb with a haunted look in his eyes. "I guess that seems more likely than visitors from another galaxy," he said. "And if they're tied in to the whole Meg Winship thing, we need to get Piper out of there now."

"Remember, Piper doesn't feel like she's in any danger from Meg," Phoebe pointed out.

"Well, maybe Piper isn't exactly thinking straight," Paige offered. "If Meg isn't mixed up in this somehow, why is her house magically shielded from us? Despite Piper's unnaturally perky state, everything is not hunky-dory."

"Well, if your professor is right, Paige," Leo said, "then Meg could somehow be involved with demons. And if that's the case—and Piper is in her hands—then Piper might well be in danger she doesn't know about. We've got to figure out what's going on, and come up with a way to get through Meg's defenses." He glanced at his watch. "We don't have long, either. The rally is just about a few hours away. I'll check with the Elders about Haywood's theory. Check the Book of Shadows again, now that we've got more to work with. And keep going through Haywood's notes to see if he has any other clues in there."

Paige nodded. "I'll make the coffee. Industrial-strength. It's gonna be a long night."

Paige listened to the coffeemaker drip its potent brew into the carafe. Her mind was racing. *Maybe we can make a potion to break through the force field,* she thought. *Could it be as easy as making this coffee? Not likely. But who knew what was likely or possible when you were a Charmed One?* The last couple of days had just been so full of activity, and the fact that Piper—the one she would normally count on to help her make sense of it all—was away from home, and possibly mixed up in the worst of it, just made it harder to concentrate and harder to deal with.

She kept seeing the face of Dr. Haywood, just before she went to make him tea, in her futile attempt to calm him down. Then it dissolved into an image of the stark white cocoon hanging in the dark warehouse, and the woman's body they had peeled from it. She had been weak, near death, but they had saved Barbara Hunsaker. Although there had been people they hadn't been able to help—even as powerful as the Charmed Ones were, they couldn't be everywhere, all the time—overall, they had made a powerful impact on the world. *Maybe that's what the Power of Three is all about,* she thought. *Maybe it does take all three of us together to really get it right.*

They would get Piper back today. Of that, she was absolutely convinced. There was no way another sun would set without her safely at home.

Before heading Up There, Leo made one last attempt to orb into Meg Winship's house. No luck. He had tried a few times before and, each time, he'd ended up with a sensation much like Paige had described.

He was more worried than he'd admitted. He knew Piper could take care of herself, but obviously she *wasn't* herself or she wouldn't have become mixed up in this. Even if she wasn't hypnotized or enchanted, unless something had been really bothering her, she wouldn't have been taken in by Meg's line. He'd have been satisfied just to talk to her. He trusted Phoebe and Paige completely, but he wanted to hear Piper's voice for himself, to see if in fact she did sound as natural as her sisters had claimed.

But he couldn't get through whatever defenses Meg had put up, and when he tried dialing the phone number of her company, all he got was a recorded message.

Since marrying Piper, he'd hated to spend a night in bed alone. He had become so used to her presence; even when she slept, just to have her comforting form in bed beside him made things better. He'd seen a lot in his time—war and tragedy, life and death, peace and pleasure. But until falling in love with Piper Halliwell, he realized, he had never truly known joy.

Now that he had found it, he didn't intend to give it up.

Tomorrow—*no, today,* he corrected, he would get Piper back. He didn't know what Meg's rally was all about, but it didn't matter. When it was over, either Piper would come with him willingly, or he would do whatever it took to free her from Meg's control and bring her home.

He knew he was, in general, a pretty determined guy. But he couldn't remember a time when he'd been more so than right now.

Piper was coming home.

Phoebe was exhausted, and she was sure that Paige was too. She couldn't deny that it had freaked her out to learn that Meg Winship was linked, in some way, to Paige's dead college teacher with the weird UFO theories. She wanted to believe Haywood was a lunatic, pure and simple. Maybe there was some kind of mass psychosis going on in the city—the madness of crowds. The more people heard stories of others who'd seen UFOs—especially the gullible types who read and believed those tabloid papers—the more they convinced themselves that they had seen them as well.

What disturbed Phoebe the most was that

Piper had somehow become mixed up in it. She seemed fine, she was lucid and articulate, but it just wasn't like Piper to get so carried away by something to the detriment of her other responsibilities. To Piper, being a Charmed One was paramount.

But maybe something else was bothering her, Phoebe realized. Piper's absence meant that she suddenly had to take on the role of oldest sister. That was a new one for her. She had been the youngest—while Prue was alive—and then middle: Both were privileged positions, for different reasons. Now, though, she found herself abruptly pushed into the one spot she had never held, or aspired to. The oldest, she understood, had to be a confidante, a confessor, a brick wall of reason and understanding and comfort. If she fell apart, where would that leave Paige? She had to be strong, had to sound like she was confident and knew what she was doing, even when that felt very far from the truth.

Delving back into the Book of Shadows—the place she'd found so many answers to so many previous questions—she hoped she was doing as good a job of it as Piper would have. She kind of thought maybe she wasn't—*there's only one Piper Halliwell, after all*—but that didn't mean she would stop trying.

By the time Bill Conason got out of the emergency room and home in a taxi—his SUV was still parked outside Play Ball—the sun was gleaming off the black glass surface of the Transamerica Pyramid. From the street outside his apartment he could see the local landmark. It towered over the Financial District, the point at its top seemingly sharp enough to cut the clouds as they passed over.

The women who'd attacked him had blackened both eyes, knocked out a tooth, bloodied his nose and, according to his X-rays, cracked a couple of ribs. Bill wondered if they'd have killed him if that car hadn't pulled into the lot. Frighteningly, he was pretty sure the answer was yes.

He had assured the doctor that he'd be filing a police report, but the more he thought about that, the less comfortable he felt trying to explain how, or why, a couple of young women in workout wear had beat the stuffing out of him. They'd made no attempt to rob him, and they'd left him with only what might have been a warning. But, given the way his ears were ringing by that point, they might have said something else altogether, or nothing at all.

As he stood on the sidewalk digging for his keys, he realized that if it was a warning, then it was one Phoebe should get as well. And he could deliver it without the punching and kicking that had accompanied his version. He left his keys in his pocket and pulled his cell phone from his jacket. He didn't know her home number, but her cell was on his phone's memory.

As it rang, he found his keys and opened the downstairs door. A moment later, her voice answered.

"I know it's early, Phoebe," he said. "It's Bill Conason."

"Bill, what's up?"

"I thought this was important enough to chance ruining your beauty sleep," he said. "I got beat up last night, pretty bad. Couple of cracked ribs, black eyes."

"Oh, no!" she said, sounding genuinely distressed. "What happened?"

"Well, here's why I thought you should know," he said. "I've been doing a little digging around about Meg Winship. I think maybe I was overheard, and when they finished with me, they warned me to keep away from her."

"From Meg Winship?" Phoebe asked.

"It's hard to be sure," he admitted. "But I think they said, 'Leave Meg alone.'"

"Are you okay? All right, stupid question. But—"

"Well, I'm not going to be running any marathons this week, but yeah," he answered. He was walking up the stairs now, two flights, in a building that had an elevator. But the elevator hadn't worked for at least six months, and of course the landlord hadn't fixed it just in case someone came home from the hospital with an ache precisely the size of his entire body. "I mean, I'm going to take as many painkillers as are allowed by law and go sleep for the rest of the day. But no permanent damage."

"That's good," she said. "And I appreciate the warning. Did you find out anything important?"

Bill put his key into the lock on his front door and turned it while he tried to decide if he'd learned anything important, and if he had, whether he'd want to share it with Phoebe. The key seemed like it turned too easily, but he hadn't really been paying attention, struggling instead with the more difficult question of how much he wanted to divulge.

When he closed the door behind himself and flipped on the light, he found out why.

Two women—not the same two as the night before, but similarly attired—stood facing him. "Hang up the phone," one commanded.

"Bill, what was that?" Phoebe asked, concerned.

He didn't answer her, but he didn't end the call either. He didn't know what was going on here, but it couldn't hurt to have someone listening in, just in case. "What are you doing in here?" he asked the women.

"Put down the phone," the taller one, in the short sweatshirt, said. "Then we can talk."

"I don't think we have anything to talk about. If you leave now, I won't have you arrested." He realized he was standing between them and the door he had just shut, but his apartment had a narrow entryway before the living room, and they were crowding the other end of it. There was no place to go but back out, and the door opened in. To get it open, he'd have to move closer to them, an idea that didn't fill him with joy.

"Bill, do you need help?" Phoebe's voice from his phone sounded desperate. "What's your address?"

The women drew closer. "If you won't put it down," the shorter one said, "we'll just have to take it away from you. And you won't like that."

Without saying anything more to Phoebe, he closed the phone and dropped it into his jacket pocket. "Look," he said hopefully, "just tell me what you want. I'm sure we can work something out. I don't have a lot of cash or anything, but—"

"We don't need your money," the shorter one said. He didn't like her tone, which managed to be both menacing and cheerful at the same time, as if she were really enjoying this.

"What, then?"

"What's the old saying?" the taller one asked. She took a step toward him, and her partner matched it. "Your money or your life?"

He tried for the door then, but as soon as he yanked it partly open, they were on him, slamming him into it, forcing it shut again. With the weight of the three of them against it, he couldn't get it open, and in a moment his hand was pulled from the knob. His injuries of the night before screamed with pain, and he could barely raise his arms to defend himself.

Mercifully, the battle was short.

Chapter

13

"Paige!" Phoebe called, dropping her cell phone. "Leo!"

Both of them orbed into her room, Paige preceding Leo by a fraction of a second. "What's wrong, Phoebe?"

"Take me here," Phoebe said, and gave Paige the address she had begged from the night city desk editor. "It's an emergency."

Paige reacted immediately, and a moment later the three of them stood outside the door to Bill Conason's apartment. The door was wide open. In the entryway, a crumpled form on the floor and wide swaths of blood on the walls painted a horrific picture.

"Bill?" Phoebe said, rushing inside. His face was bloody and pulpy, looking more like raw hamburger than the thoughtful but ambitious reporter she knew, and his joints protruded from his collapsed shape at odd angles. She put her fingers against his neck, ignoring the blood, but felt no pulse. "Leo," she said, her voice shaking. "Can you?"

Leo stepped forward, and she moved aside to give him room. With his Whitelighter powers, Leo could heal the injured. He knelt beside Bill for a moment, his face furrowed with concern, and put his hands on the fallen reporter. But then he looked up at Phoebe, his eyes filled with sorrow. "We're too late to help him."

Phoebe felt tears spring to her eyes. She had known he was dead from the instant they'd arrived, but hearing Leo pronounce it that way removed all hope.

"Do you know what happened?" Paige asked, stroking Phoebe's arm with sisterly concern.

"He called me," Phoebe said, wiping her eyes with her fingers. "It sounded like he'd just walked in and there was someone waiting for him. I couldn't hear very well, but it sounded like a female voice. Then he went away. I got his address from the paper, and that's when I called you."

"Why did he call you?" Leo asked. "Who is he?"

Phoebe moved away from the entry, scoping out the rest of the apartment on the off-chance that Bill's attacker hadn't left yet. Bill's place was small and crowded, but still neatly organized. "His name is Bill Conason," she told the others. "He's a reporter at the *Bay Mirror*. I asked him some stuff about the UFOs, and I guess at the end he was investigating the Meg Winship angle. He said he was attacked last night, by someone warning him away from Meg. He wanted to warn me, just in case."

"So maybe whoever attacked him last night wanted to finish the job," Leo suggested.

"And Piper is still with Meg," Paige pointed out. "Those other women we saw there might be Innocents too. We have to get them out of there!"

"Unless you've figured a way to get past the force field, that's still not an option," Leo reminded her. "The big rally is today. They should be safe at least until that's over. Until then, Meg seems to need them."

"I guess we know what we're doing today," Phoebe said. She made an anonymous call to the police on Bill's home phone, to report his murder, then wiped it clean of her fingerprints. Ensuring that there were no other surfaces they'd touched, she took one last look at her murdered friend and asked Paige to orb them home.

Back at the Manor, they tried to formulate a plan. "I wish we knew how to prepare for this," Paige said.

"Me too," Leo said. "Even the Elders are at a loss. They say there seems to be something big in the offing—there's a huge amount of mystical energy swirling around the city—but they can't pinpoint who's behind it, or what it's all about."

"Well, it looks pretty much guaranteed that Meg Winship is behind it," Phoebe speculated. "Since Bill was warned away from her."

"That's what bothers me," Paige agreed. "If Meg's up to something big and bad, how is she going to implicate Piper? Does she want her powers, or to keep us from having the Power of Three? Does she even know Piper's got powers? We've got to get answers, and there's only one way to get them."

"Except we can't get there from here," Phoebe lamented. "We can't get into Meg's estate. But we know she'll be at the rally today, and the rally's open to the public. So we'll just have to get to her then."

"If we can," Paige said. "What if she's been working with demons somehow? Maybe she's even a demon herself."

"She's no demon," Leo said. "The Elders knew that much. She's a mortal."

"Okay, so we see what we can find out until rally time." Paige was building steam. "Shake a few trees, rattle some lesser demons cages, if necessary. This chick and her perky pink joggers are goin' down."

Phoebe smiled and gave her sister a high five. "Works for me."

The Charmed Ones didn't always know where demons might be found—they had a tendency, after all, to vanquish the ones they were aware of. But like anybody else, demons had patterns, habits, and were often predictable. It took a few tries, but finally they found an Ecari Demon in the Filmore District, stalking a woman as she hurried home after a late shift at work. His head was bald and smooth, his face almost handsome, his form—clad in a loose, belted shirt and pants, almost like a karate gi, of a dark plum color— broad and muscular. In his bearing there was a hint of nobility, as if this demon were royalty of some kind, used to commanding obedience.

"Fancy," Phoebe whispered.

"Almost too bad we'll have to get him dirty," Paige teased.

They waited until the woman was safely around a corner, then emerged from their hiding places. "Hey, homely," Phoebe said.

The Ecari whirled on them, his clawed hands closing into fists. "Who dares—?"

Phoebe and Paige stood a few paces apart, facing him. "You might have heard of us," Phoebe said. "The Charmed Ones?"

He studied them for a moment, during which he did not relax. Every muscle in his body was coiled, ready to fight or flee. "I had heard that you were three."

"We are," Paige replied. "But we don't need all three of us to deal with someone as minor-league as you. Even two is probably overkill."

"You dare to mock me?" the demon complained.

"We not only dare," Phoebe said with a grin, "we take great pleasure from it."

He glanced over his shoulder briefly, as if confirming that he had already lost his prize. Then he turned back, a resolute expression on his face. "I think you bluff," he declared. "I believe you have not attacked because you fear me."

"We have not attacked," Phoebe countered, "because we want information. If all we wanted was to vanquish you, you'd already be gone. We'd rather find out what you know."

The Ecari made a move like a shrug, shifting his shoulders—but instead of following it through, he suddenly lowered his right shoulder and dove at Paige, his clawed hands extended like daggers slicing through the night. Paige orbed out and reappeared behind him. He stumbled, expecting to encounter resistance where there was none.

"Boo," Paige said as he turned this way and that, looking for her.

He let out a low growl and swung at her again. This time Phoebe intervened, moving in with a quick one-two punch to his torso. The claws narrowly missed her, but her own blows landed hard. The Ecari grunted with pain and fell back a couple of steps. Phoebe closed again, to follow up, but one of its flailing hands caught her, knocking her away.

Before the demon could press his attack, Paige distracted him with two fast blows to the back of his head. When he spun around to face her, she had already vanished from that spot. The Ecari blinked in momentary confusion, unable to keep up with her.

Phoebe took advantage of the confusion, regaining her footing and launching into a spin. She let loose with two hard kicks as she did—the first catching the demon in the gut, and the second, as he began to fold in on himself, smashing into his jaw. By the time she ended her spin, the Ecari was on the ground, a trickle of silvery blood running from his mouth. He put one of his hands up to his lips and drew it away, wet and sticky.

"You could make this easier on yourself," Phoebe suggested. "It should be obvious by now that you can't hope to beat us."

"You are . . . formidable," the demon agreed, sounding reluctant but resigned.

"Then let's stop fighting and start talking," Paige said.

"I take it you have a particular topic in mind?"

"You take it right," Phoebe said. "You ever heard of Meg Winship?"

"You have no idea how little the affairs of humans interest me," the Ecari said with a snarl. "Except for food or sport, humans mean nothing to me." The demon had a tone of superiority in its voice that infuriated Phoebe.

"You're talking to two of them, so you might

want to choose your words carefully," she said.

"Charmed Ones are not human," the demon shot back.

"Of course we are," Paige said. "I mean, we're witches. But we're human, too. That's kind of the point."

"Bah!" The demon spat on the ground. "You are by definition more than human. Mere humans could not survive against me in battle, even for a moment."

"You're getting off-topic," Phoebe said. "We want to know about Meg Winship."

"I have heard the name," the Ecari admitted. "But I know nothing more than that."

"What about UFO sightings around town?" Paige prompted. "Do you know anything about those?"

"Very little." The demon seemed upset by his own lack of information. "Demonic manifestation of some kind, but like nothing I have experienced before."

"So they are demons?" Paige pressed.

"I did not say that," the Ecari corrected her. "I said 'demonic manifestation.' I do not believe that they are demons—merely an indication of demonic activity."

"There must be some kind of talk in the demonic world," Phoebe said. "Rumors, or something."

The Ecari shrugged. "Rumors are worthless. Everyone knows something is imminent, but no one knows what. Every demon you speak to has some other theory. None of it makes any sense. The Ecari are above all that. We exist, we feed, we amuse ourselves. We don't concern ourselves with foolish talk."

"Well, aren't you special?" Paige asked. "Too bad you don't know something useful—it just might convince us not to vanquish you."

The Ecari's eyes widened at the word. "Vanquish? But you said—"

"We never said we wouldn't," Phoebe reminded him. "We said we wanted to talk. We've talked. You don't know anything. You really think we're just going to let you go, so you can feed on Innocents?"

"What if I could tell you . . ." The demon let his sentence trail off.

"Tell us what?"

He shrugged again. "Nothing. There is nothing I can tell you, because I know nothing about these manifestations, or this person you ask about. All I can do is suggest that you're wasting your time. No one knows any more than me."

Paige almost felt bad about vanquishing him, but then she thought about the woman he'd been trailing, who, it appeared, he'd been about to have for breakfast.

After that, she didn't feel bad at all.

Back in the kitchen of Halliwell Manor, they told Leo what they had been able to learn.

"Not a thing," Phoebe reported. "We questioned half a dozen demons. It was a good night's work, vanquishing-wise. But now I'm even more exhausted than before, and we still don't have a clue."

"It's like, everyone knows something's brewing," Paige added. "And a couple of them even seemed to think Meg was at the center of it all. But none of them know what it is. If she's working with any demons, it's no one from around here."

Leo nodded. "Which is pretty much what the Elders came up with. Something big is in the works. Meg is involved. But what, how, why . . . all those things are just blanks. Which makes it that much more difficult for us to deal with."

"Yeah," Paige agreed. "Since we really have no idea what we'll be up against, it's hard."

"We've been in that situation before," Leo reminded them. "We'll just have to be ready for anything they might throw at us."

"And keep in mind that they're killers," Phoebe added. "They won't hesitate to take us out if they need to, I'm sure."

"They could have attacked us when we were at Meg's," Paige said. "But they didn't."

"I'm sure Piper would have freaked out if she had seen that," Phoebe speculated. "We weren't a threat to Meg at the time, so she wouldn't have wanted to risk losing control of Piper."

"I think you're right," Leo said, sitting down

at the table with them. "The question remains, does she need Piper because of Piper's powers? Or is it some other reason?"

"If we had Piper with us, the Power of Three could kick her butt, magical defenses or no," Paige said. "But as long as she has one of us working with her, the rest can't get in."

Leo cocked his head, a thought forming. "I wonder if the rest of us can't get in *because* Piper is there. Could Meg somehow be using Piper's power against us?"

A horrible idea crossed Phoebe's mind. "What if things go bad during the rally?" she asked. "What if we need to fight Meg, and find ourselves up against Piper?"

"Then we make sure Piper doesn't get hurt," Leo said simply. "We remember that Meg is a killer—or at least, that her supporters are willing to kill on her behalf. And we take no chances. There has to be a way to get Piper out of there without being hurt."

Phoebe hoped he was right, and not just indulging in wishful thinking because he was worried about his wife. She was worried, too, of course. She had been absolutely convinced that Piper was fine, that for whatever reason she had chosen to stay and work for Meg. But if Meg had somehow brainwashed these women into murdering for her, could they be sure that Piper wasn't similarly controlled? And if she was, how far could they go in defending themselves against her? Of the three of them, Piper's powers had the potential to be most destructive, and if she wasn't fully in command of her own abilities, then she could be a fearsome opponent. Especially if they were trying hard not to hurt her at the same time that she was trying to finish them.

The day started early for Meg Winship. Anita, her personal assistant, buzzed her awake at six. She got out of bed, changed into exercise wear— Meg Winship signature-brand, of course—and went down to her private gym for a forty-minute workout. After that, a shower and some breakfast, watching the morning news on three TVs at once. Along with the rest of the world's violence and small tragedies were reports of a local journalist's murder. What pleased Meg, though, was that all three channels mentioned the rally later at the Presidio.

Breakfast completed, she paged Anita. The woman joined her, crisp and clean in a charcoal business suit with white pinstripes, and together they walked through the house, checking on progress.

"Is everything ready on site?" Meg asked.

Anita nodded once. Everything about her was no-nonsense and professional. "The chairs are being set up right now," she said. "We wanted to wait until the ground dried so they wouldn't sink unevenly. The stage was constructed last night. I gave it the once-over this morning. It's exactly to specifications."

"Good," Meg said, gracing her assistant with a smile. "Security?"

"Sasha is on site," Anita said, naming the head of Meg's private security force. "She's got her people training the volunteers." Normally, Meg's security team only had to safeguard the house, and a couple of trusted officers went with her when she traveled anywhere. But this rally was the biggest thing Meg had ever tried to pull off, and they needed volunteers to help protect the perimeter, as well as for crowd control.

They stopped in at the workroom where Piper Halliwell and some others had been assembling the goody bags for all attendees. The bags had been finished and taken to the site, so the room was now empty. Meg found herself hoping Piper's sisters didn't try to make trouble at the event. She was pretty sure they had been reassured that Piper was fine, but that didn't mean they were finished snooping around.

If they did, they'd find that Meg Winship was ready for them. Nothing had been left to chance here—nothing could be. This day was a culmination for Meg, the last rung on the ladder from what she had been—a simple, suggestible schoolgirl, unsure of what she wanted from life—to what she was becoming.

After today, everyone would know the name Meg Winship. And fear it. Power—the kind that

moved nations, and made worlds tremble—
would be in her grasp. Meg's message wasn't
just talk, after all. Everyone could improve themselves, choose their own destiny.

It was just that most people didn't know the
extent to which they could do so. But Meg did.
Having found out, she couldn't allow herself to
be anything less than her ultimate self. She had
to be her ideal Meg—and her ideal made the
dreams of most humans look miserly by com-
parison. Many—possibly most—women would
be content to have achieved what she had, to be
young and beautiful and rich.

Meg knew there was much more that could
be achieved. And because it could be, it had to
be. Simple as that. She turned back to Anita. "It's
a very important day," she said.

"Yes," Anita agreed. "Very important."

"Everything changes, after today," Meg told
her. Anita didn't know the real extent to which
that was true, and she wouldn't be told until it
happened. "Everything."

"There's never been anyone like you, Meg,"
Anita said. "And there probably never will be
again. Your name will be immortal, after this."

That's the general idea, Meg thought. *Not that I
care what anyone thinks after I'm gone. But I want
everyone to know it while I'm here.*

Chapter

14

Darryl knew from Carter Haywood's phone records that he had called Meg Winship the day he died. It had been a short phone call, and there was no guarantee that he had actually talked to Winship. But her office had been very unhelpful, refusing to allow Darryl to speak to her. They said it was because she was busy getting ready for the big rally, but the fact that he was investigating a homicide should have carried some weight. The lack of cooperation only increased his suspicions.

It didn't really matter. He knew she'd be at the rally today. He'd wait until she was off-stage and then he'd have his conversation with her. And if that wasn't enough, she'd return to the station with him and they'd have it there. Entirely too many San Franciscans had been dying lately, and while he could only link

Winship to one—so far—that was a good starting point.

The latest victim was a reporter who'd worked at the *Bay Mirror*. Darryl hadn't caught the case, and didn't know many of the details yet. But he planned to talk to the responsible detective and he'd pay close attention. Phoebe Halliwell worked at the *Bay Mirror*. So did hundreds of other people, of course. But none of them were Halliwells. Trouble followed the Halliwells around like a lost puppy, and if there was a chance that this reporter's murder was connected to Phoebe—or to Meg Winship—Darryl wanted to know about it.

Sasha Wilensky's family moved from the Soviet Union to the United States when she was just an infant. The daughter of Soviet Olympians, Sasha grew up tall and strong. By the time she was eighteen she had been bodybuilding competitively for two years.

After college, a stint in the marines was followed by recruitment for the United States Secret Service. She stayed in that position, part of the First Lady's security detail, until that family left office and Sasha retired from the Service and went into private practice, running security for Meg Winship. She had worked for Meg for two years now. Compared with her previous position, the job was pretty routine, for the most part.

Recently, though, things had changed. Meg

had been asking her to do things she had never asked before—things that would have shocked her, once.

Not now. Now, she found that she was essentially unshockable. Whatever Meg asked of her, she agreed to without hesitation. At the back of her mind, sometimes, was a niggling sense that something was wrong, that she was doing things, carrying out orders, that seemed suspect to her. But that feeling never lasted more than a couple of seconds. By the time Sasha was in motion, carrying out the order, it had gone away completely.

Never before had she had the sole responsibility for such a large event. Her usual staff of thirty was supplemented by a hundred volunteers, women in matching pink T-shirts. The event site, a grassy field in San Francisco's Presidio, was huge, with a thousand plastic chairs set up in neat rows, and a specially constructed stage for Meg. Sasha had placed volunteers at the entrance, at the stage doors, surrounding the front of the stage, at the rear driveway through which Meg would enter, and in each aisle between the four sections of seats. Professionals were also situated on the driveway and at various points around the site, to assist the volunteers should anything unexpected happen. All the professionals and select volunteers were linked by headsets. As things were being set up, there was so much headset chatter that it was giving Sasha a headache.

Now she sat at her temporary command post, a folding table set up inside the stage construction, massaging her temples and trying to imagine what might go wrong. Thinking of the worst that could happen was the most important part of her job. Someone could sneak a gun in, attempt to assassinate Meg. To forestall that, everyone admitted would come through a metal detector and have any handbags or backpacks searched at the entrance. No one with a close-up weapon, such as a knife, would get near enough to Meg to use it. She was also worried about Meg's fans being carried away in the enthusiasm of the moment and rushing the stage. The biggest, strongest women on the staff and the largest of the volunteers were stationed at the foot of the stage to discourage that. Some things, like the air space overhead, Sasha simply couldn't control, but there would be operatives in the wings of the stage on both sides, ready to hustle Meg away if anything unexpected happened.

She knew, of course, that chances were there would be no incidents at all. This was a crowd who admired Meg Winship, and probably the most dangerous thing Meg would face would be a zealous fan looking for an autograph or a hug. But this was the biggest and most heavily promoted public appearance of Meg's career, and Sasha would take it as seriously as she would have a public speech by the First Lady.

She had taken her fine, platinum hair out of

the severe ponytail she favored to rub her temples, trying to ease the building headache there, and was just putting it back when Anita, Meg's personal assistant, showed up. Anita was crisply attired, as usual, and smiling casually. Under her arm Anita carried a red leather portfolio.

"How's it going?" Anita asked her.

"Everything's under control," Sasha said, trying to breathe through her mouth. "Do you want to go over Meg's entrance again?"

Anita shook her head. "No, I think we've got it covered," she replied. She opened the portfolio and took out a couple of photographs. When she put them down on the table, Sasha recognized the angles—they were taken by surveillance cameras on the estate, one at the front gate and another inside the main hallway. They showed two attractive young women.

"Who are they?" Sasha asked.

"According to Meg," Anita said, "potential trouble. Keep an eye out for them today. If they show up, get rid of them—discreetly, of course, and permanently if necessary."

That little stray thought at the back of her mind tickled her, like a hair that escaped from her ponytail and worried at the back of her neck. But as quickly as it had come up, it vanished. "You're sure about this?" she asked Anita. She knew they both understood what she was asking Meg's assistant to confirm.

"A hundred percent."

"Very well," she said. She glanced at the photos again, and then slid them across the table, back toward Anita.

"You don't want to keep them?" Anita asked.

Sasha looked into Anita's eyes until the woman had picked up the pictures and put them back in her portfolio. "I never saw them," she said. "If I were you, I would destroy them—and any record of their existence."

She held Anita's gaze until the light of understanding dawned in her eyes. "Got it," Anita said at last. "Consider it done."

"I will."

Anita left then, and Sasha watched her trim figure until she was out of sight. The woman hadn't seemed particularly surprised or put out about the order she was passing along, Sasha realized. She wondered what else Meg might have commanded that she had never heard about.

Meg Winship rode alone in the back of the limo, reveling in the last hours of solitude before she had to address a mass audience. She was prepared, rehearsed, pumped up. Her whole body seemed to tingle with the anticipation of what was to come. The excitement and enthusiasm of a crowd invigorated her, and this would be the biggest crowd yet. She could hardly wait for the sensation of standing on the stage, soaking up the applause and adoration of hundreds of women.

And that would just be the beginning.

She had told no one what the day really meant. Not even Anita, to whom she was as close as any other person on Earth. No one else would understand—at least, at first. After the fact, they would have to understand, because it would all be right there in front of them, in the open. But until they saw it for their own eyes, they wouldn't be able to comprehend what Meg knew.

She almost wished Carter Haywood could be here to see it. He had been too timid to see the truth, to carry his findings the extra step that was needed to bring them to fruition. Once he had finally figured out the true meaning of his discovery, he had panicked. The only reason he wouldn't be here as an honored guest was that he wouldn't have gone along with it. He would have objected, and tried to prevent the full realization of his own efforts.

Meg didn't understand that kind of weakness. She didn't understand weakness at all— what was life about, if not the pursuit of strength: physical, emotional, mental? Allowing weakness to rule was the same as giving up. It was surrendering to something less than one could be.

She alone was willing and able to go all the way, to take Carter's research, and her own independent findings, to their ultimate conclusion. Carter had been correct, at least in his later

assumptions, after he'd got over believing that
UFOs were evidence of visitors from some other
planet in our universe.

The fact was, they were indicators of life on
another plane of reality, one separated from this
reality by the thinnest of veils. Sure, they tried to
come through, but could only send their avatars.
These entities could not interact with Earth, or
influence it, at first, and they took the forms that
humans expected to see, and could emotionally
cope with.

But Meg, building on the groundbreaking
research Carter had done, discovered a way to
reach out to them, through ritual magic, and to
strengthen them. With the power they gave Meg,
she had found she could influence the minds of
women throughout the region. At first, she had
to manifest her power in concrete ways, which
would be visible to her victims, so she had
chosen to use the avatars to do so. Their shapes
were almost comforting to the women she
approached—not everyday shapes, but not completely unknown, either. Finally, as her power
had grown, fed by the admiration of her followers, she had been able to stop using the shapes of
the avatars and could simply reach out via TV,
radio, or personal appearances. This was how
she had reached Piper Halliwell, bringing her
into the inner circle and therefore eliminating
any threat the Charmed Ones might pose to her
plan. The Others told her, through their inter-

dimensional communication process, about the three witches and the likelihood that they would interfere if they could. They also taught her how to create an impenetrable barrier around herself. The much-vaunted Power of Three might have been able to break through, but without Piper, the remaining sisters wouldn't have a chance.

Using the techniques taught her by the Others, she controlled those around her while building up her own fan base throughout the city. And conversely, by channeling the energies her fans spent in the pursuit of exercise, she made herself stronger. Today, it would finally culminate. She would lead her most dedicated fans in a specific ritual she had created. Their combined strength, channeled through her, would rip open the veil and allow the Others free entrance to this plane. Here, with powers unknown on Earth, the Others would seem god-like, and as their prophet on this plane, Meg would sit at their right hand, all the power and influence she had ever wanted and deserved at her disposal.

Carter Haywood could have shared in it, if he hadn't been so weak. Meg was unwilling to suffer weakness from him, or anyone else. After today, she wouldn't have to, ever again.

She leaned back into the plush leather seat of the limousine that bore her inexorably toward her ultimate fate, toward the fate of the world.

After today, everything would change. The

world would be undone and remade, just as muscle was built by breaking down tissue and building it up again.

Meg Winship would create the Earth's ideal self.

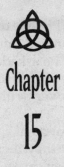

Chapter
15

Paige thought time had never passed more slowly.

Piper was out there, with Meg Winship, who they now had reason to suspect was behind at least two murders, and somehow connected to the rash of apparent UFO abductions that had plagued the city in recent weeks. And until Meg's rally started, she, Phoebe, and Leo couldn't get to Piper, couldn't break through whatever mystical barrier kept them apart from their sister.

With no help from any of the usual sources, or even the demons they tracked down, they had prepared some all-encompassing spells and potions, since they didn't know precisely what they'd be up against. Now it was just a matter of getting to the rally and doing what they could to get Piper away from Meg's clutches and bring her safely back home.

She met Leo and Phoebe on the stairs, as they headed out. He arched an eyebrow at her. "Ready to rumble?" he asked.

"More than," she answered.

"Let's get this over with and bring Piper home," Phoebe said.

Leo nodded. "Sounds like a plan."

Ascertaining that they were as ready as they were going to be, they drove to the Presidio and found a parking place a few blocks away. When they arrived, they saw what must have been hundreds of women streaming into a fenced area through a gate. The women were young and old, fit and out of shape, of every color and race found on the planet. Most of them wore workout clothes of some kind, many Meg Winship signature brands. Besides their choice of clothing, the thing they had in common was that they all looked cheerful and glad to be where they were. They chatted and laughed, clearly enjoying one another's company and looking forward to the event they were about to attend.

"The pink shirts are the muscle," Leo said, sizing up the situation.

"Yeah, I think you're right," Paige said. "And there's something else I notice."

"What's that?" Leo asked.

"You're not going to be able to go in there with us."

She watched Leo looking at the crowd, the realization dawning on him. Only women were going inside. A few men straggled around the exterior perimeter, which was walled off by tall canvas panels, like sails on the grass. The men may have been husbands or boyfriends, Paige speculated, here to show their support—or their concern—for their loved ones, but it quickly became clear that the rally was a females-only occasion and men were definitely not invited inside.

"Looks like you're right," Leo agreed. He crossed his arms over his chest. "I could go in drag."

"Nobody wants to see that," Phoebe said quickly.

"He's joking, Phoebe," Paige said. "You *are* joking, right?"

Leo shrugged. "Mostly. But I'm worried about Piper."

"Then trust us to bring her out," Phoebe said.

"Besides, you can orb in if we need you," Paige promised.

"I'll be waiting."

"You'd better go now," Paige suggested. "You're kind of calling attention to us."

"Okay, okay," Leo said. "Call at the first sign of trouble." He wandered away, leaving Paige and Phoebe by themselves on the grassy lawn.

"Shall we?" Phoebe asked.

"Ready when you are." They linked arms and joined the river of women going inside the enclosed area. At the entrance they passed through a metal detector, but they hadn't brought purses, so they weren't searched. The metal detector couldn't detect the small glass potion vials they carried in their pockets.

Inside, chairs had been arranged in four sections of widely spaced rows. The rows near the front were already full, and seats were filling quickly even toward the back. "Good turnout," Paige said. "This is going to be standing-room-only in no time."

"Maybe we're in the wrong business," Phoebe said sarcastically.

"You're right," Paige shot back, with equal sarcasm. "Instead of being good witches, we should be evil fitness gurus. Better hours, and the fringe benefits are great."

Intent on not calling any more attention to themselves than they already had, Paige and Phoebe sat quietly, scanning the crowd for any sign of Piper and watching the rest of the women filing into the arena. As outside, the women seemed for the most part to be in a celebratory mood, as if something they'd been looking forward to for a long time had finally come to pass. Paige found herself almost envying them. She loved her sisters and the life of a Charmed One, but it wouldn't be a bad thing to be so happy about something external, something that didn't involve any effort of her own, but was as simple as finding excitement in a glimpse of a celebrity. Her concerns—saving

Innocents, saving the world, that kind of thing—
were much more complex, and they weighed
heavily on her shoulders. Finding something to
get excited about that was less stressful would
be a happy thing, and she resolved that, when
this was over and they had Piper back, she
would make an attempt to do just that.

First things first, though, she thought. And first
was finding Piper. She turned in her plastic chair
and shielded her eyes with her hand against the
bright, warm sun, searching the crowd behind
them just in case Piper had come in while her
attention was toward the front. As she did,
though, an almost electric buzz passed through
the crowd. *She's here!* Paige thought, caught up
in the group's excitement in spite of herself. She
turned around again, facing the front, trying to
see what everyone was reacting to.

Behind the stage area, Paige could see a
glimpse of a long black limousine. She figured
that must have been the car bringing Meg,
which should mean that Piper was on the
premises too. She started to lean toward Phoebe
to whisper to her, when a deafening roar went
up from the crowd. The vocal roar gave way to
applause, loud and sustained, and then women
were leaving their chairs, standing, arching on
tiptoes to see over one another.

And then Meg was on the stage, striding out as
if with grand purpose, raising her hands to the
crowd, and what had been merely deafening

graduated to ear-destroying, the thunder of bomb blasts at close range. Meg Winship's smile, magnified on giant screens, was electric, her presence stirring the faithful to new heights of appreciation. Paige and Phoebe were on their feet, craning their necks to see over other women, looking, in their search for their sister, just like everyone else in the crowd.

After what must have been five minutes of soaking up the adulation, Meg made sit-down motions with her hands, bowed, clapped at the audience, and eventually got people back into their seats. A hush fell across the whole arena as everyone waited for her to speak.

"Do you see her?" Paige whispered.

"Not yet," Phoebe replied.

"*Shhh!*" several women around them shushed.

"Thank you all so much for that wonderful welcome," Meg said, prompting another upswell of applause and whoops from the audience. This one didn't last long, though, and then Meg continued, her voice amplified by giant speakers at the edges of the stage. "Thank you. It's so great to be here with all of you today, on this glorious San Francisco day. We are going to have a great time this afternoon, and you ladies are the reason why."

Again, a round of applause from the enthusiastic audience. *This woman could stand up there and read a credit card bill and they'd cheer her,* Paige thought.

"You sound like you're happy," Meg said when

it had died down. "Are you happy today?" Another sustained burst of cheering. "That's great," she went on. "It's great because that's what today is all about. What my life is all about, for that matter. I want you—I want all of us—to be happy, healthy, and whole. It's not just about being fit, it's not just about having material things—it's certainly not about having a man, or the right man, or the right woman for that matter . . . I guess I should say the right life partner. It's the whole package— happy, healthy, and whole—and it doesn't come from any external factor, or any set of external factors. It can only come from within. It comes from you—making the right choices for your body, for your mind, and for your spirit. It comes from you accepting the Meg Winship challenge to become the Ideal You!"

This statement prompted an outburst almost equal to the one that had accompanied Meg's first appearance on stage. Paige found her mood starting to turn—the more excited the audience got, the more turned off she became. Sure, Meg's message was a positive one—one that Paige agreed with, in fact. But the way the audience reacted to her every word was what disturbed Paige. There was no disagreement, no real thought being given to anything Meg said—just robotic acceptance. The crowd cheered and clapped in absolute unison, nearly identical smiles pasted onto their faces. Paige found the whole thing a bit cultlike, and it scared her. She caught Phoebe's eye, and her sister looked just as uncomfortable as she felt. *We've really got to find Piper,* she thought, *and get out of here.*

"I'm sorry, sir," the woman in the pink T-shirt told Darryl Morris. "You can't go in there. Men aren't invited to this event."

"Number one, that's gender discrimination," Darryl said. "And number two, I'm not here as a man, I'm here as an officer of the San Francisco Police Department. Now please let me through."

Four other women, identically attired, closed ranks behind the first one. "I'm sorry, sir," she said again. "I've been told that there are no exceptions to the rule."

"I'm telling you that if you don't get out of my way, I can charge you with obstruction of justice," Darryl warned. "Just don't make things any more difficult on yourself, and let me in."

"You heard her," one of the other women said. Darryl saw more pink shirts coming their way from behind the barricades. Someone had put out the alert. "We don't want you in here."

"This is a public park and a public event," Darryl said, trying to remain reasonable. "You don't have the right to keep me out."

"We're at our legal capacity," another woman put in. "If we let you in, we'd be breaking the law."

"I'm just one person," Darryl said, realizing even as he said it that it was a weak argument. If he hadn't been trying to get inside he would have made the exact same argument she had: Capacity was capacity, and "just one person" was one person too many.

Now, though, there were a dozen women flanking the first one. They glared at him, arms folded over their chests, grim expressions on their faces. He could bully past them and maybe start a fight, maybe even have to injure some of them or draw his weapon. He didn't want that. For one thing, it would make the department look bad. And for another, on the other side of the barricade were a couple thousand more women who wouldn't be happy to see him.

There were times when discretion was, in fact, the better part of valor. And there were times when a cop just needed a lot of backup. This was looking like one of those times. Darryl wanted to get inside, wanted to hear Meg Winship's talk, to try to figure out what her game was. But it didn't look like doing so was going to be easy.

He retreated with a smile and a shrug, trying to look like he was giving up. But when he got back to his car, he called for a riot squad to come to the scene. Just in case. Better to have them here and not need them than need them and have them somewhere else. He didn't think things were necessarily going to go bad.

But if they did, he wanted to be ready.

Chapter

16

Meg Winship encouraged her audience to get out of their chairs to join her in some stretching exercises. "We always warm up first—right, ladies?" Meg asked.

The answer, from a thousand throats, was a resounding "Yes!" Fast-paced music began to blare from dozens of speakers. As one, the women left their chairs and sat on the ground, mimicking Meg's movements. Phoebe and Paige went along so as not to stand out. As they did, though, Phoebe caught a glimpse of a familiar ponytail in a taped-off, reserved seating section a dozen or so rows ahead of them that she hadn't seen before. Legs spread in a wide V, fingers on toes, trying to touch her knee with her head, Phoebe whispered, "Paige! Piper is about twelve rows up, dead ahead."

She saw Paige angle for a peek when they

rose up to switch legs, and when they bent forward again, Paige said, "I see her too."

"We have to move up," Phoebe said.

"How?"

"I don't know," Phoebe answered. "But we have to get her."

"I know that," Paige shot back. "It's just . . . I don't see a lot of people changing seats, you know? They'll notice us."

"Well, we have to figure out something soon or we'll lose her in this crowd," Phoebe said. People were starting to shush them again because they were talking while Meg counted out the seconds. *As if you can't count for yourselves,* she thought angrily.

They agreed to wait until the stretching exercises were done, when presumably people would be on their feet again and they wouldn't be as obvious walking toward the front. Phoebe had to admit that Meg knew what she was doing—from going along with the warm-up, she felt limber and loose. Her heart was pumping, her breathing quickened, and she felt fresh and ready for anything.

Meg called for the audience to stand and prepare for a real workout, and, with a great cheer, they did so. As the women began to move in concert with Meg and the pounding music, Phoebe and Paige slipped from their row.

The routine Meg led the audience through was a strange one, Phoebe noted. She had never seen anything quite like it before, and since she and Paige were walking down the aisle between sections, she had a clear view of the process. With both hands in the air, palms out, Meg and her followers raised one foot high, knee bent, then stomped it down hard, shifting weight to that leg and throwing their hips to that side. Bringing the hands down and shaking them, they repeated the leg-and-hip move with the other side. Then two quick steps forward, two back, and into the same routine again. Meg did it all with a delighted smile, and Phoebe noticed that most of the women in the audience copied that part as well.

"This must be on the video," Paige said as they made their way down the aisle, trying to be discreet but still heard over the music and the stomping. "Everyone is exactly in step."

Phoebe realized she was right. A thousand women, give or take, and every right foot came down at the same precise, earthshaking moment. The hands moved in perfect unison, the hips thrust, the steps up and back. The Rockettes couldn't have done it better, and Phoebe was sure these women had never all practiced together. "It's kind of weird," she replied. "It's so . . . perfect."

Paige nodded, but didn't speak. None of the women exercising seemed aware of their presence, but their aisle was off to the left of center stage, and Phoebe noted that a woman in the wings on the far side, standing with arms crossed in a pink T-shirt, was glaring hard at them. Then the woman turned away slightly and held her hand over her ear.

"We've been spotted," Phoebe said quietly.

"We're almost there," Paige observed. She was right; the reserved section was only a couple of rows down. But Piper was in the middle of her row, so they'd have to not only get through the tape but past a dozen women shaking their hands and hips and stepping forward and back.

When they reached Piper's row, two things happened simultaneously. Meg changed her routine, and a line of pink shirt–clad women started up the aisle toward them with resolute expressions on their faces. The new routine was faster than the last, a running-in-place thing with added fillips—arms waving up and down as in jumping jacks, heads flopping right to left like a dancer in that old *Charlie Brown Christmas* TV special. The whole thing looked comical to Phoebe, and she wondered how Meg could ever have been taken seriously with such bizarre routines.

The women coming toward them didn't look so comical, though. Phoebe grabbed Paige's arm, and they ducked under the tape, starting down the row to where Piper was moving in concert with all the rest. The exercising women they passed barely glanced at them, but managed to avoid hitting them with flailing arms and pumping knees.

When they reached Piper, she gave them a big smile, but didn't stop moving. "Hi, guys," she said brightly. "Are you having fun? You should be working out with us!"

"Piper," Phoebe replied sharply. "We need to get out of here, now!"

"Not now," Piper objected. "We've just started."

"But Piper," Paige chimed in, "Leo is really worried about you. And we've found out some stuff about Meg that—"

"Meg is my friend," Piper declared, cutting Paige off mid-stream. She never lost her smile or her rhythm. "And she's a wonderful human being."

"I'm sure she is," Phoebe lied, trying to keep her sister humored long enough to get her away. She turned to Paige. "Orb us out!"

Paige closed her eyes and gritted her teeth. "I can't," she said. "We're blocked here too."

Great, Phoebe thought. *Which means that Leo can't get in, either.*

"Piper, come on," she pleaded. "Please, just come with us."

"No!" Piper snapped, though the smile remained plastered in place. "Not until we're done here."

Phoebe felt Paige tugging on her arm, and she turned to see what was the matter. "We have company," Paige whispered urgently. At the end of the row, the women in pink had massed and were moving inexorably toward them.

"Piper!" Phoebe said again, trying to grab her sister's arms to get her to stop moving even for a moment and pay attention to the importance of the moment. Piper shook her off, though, missing the beat for a fraction of a second. When she did, the smile turned to an angry scowl, but it passed so quickly, it might almost have been an illusion, a trick of the sunlight. As soon as Piper was in tune with the other women, the smile reappeared on her face as if it had never left.

Without a word, Meg shifted routines again, and Piper and the rest of the audience flowed seamlessly into the new one. Phoebe had to dodge Piper's right arm, which shot out suddenly in a kind of boxing move. "Piper, watch out!" she complained.

"If you'd join us, you wouldn't have to worry," Piper pointed out.

Phoebe supposed that was true, as far as it went—except that if she joined them, she'd worry about her own mental health. "Piper, those women are coming to get us," Phoebe said anxiously.

"Oh, that's because you're not supposed to be in this row," Piper explained. "This section is reserved for volunteers."

"They were coming for us before we got to this section, though," Phoebe pointed out.

"Well, they're Meg's security crew," Piper observed, "so maybe you did something wrong."

"I think the only thing we've done wrong is to

try to help our sister," Paige commented. "And they don't look like they're here to talk things out."

Phoebe stole another glance at the security detail, threading down the row. Paige was right: The women in the pink shirts were mean looking, with frowns on their faces, and enormous muscles on their arms. The only chance to avoid a confrontation now, she knew, was if Piper would agree to leave, they could go the other direction down the row, and then hurry to an exit. Piper, though, still gave no indication of being willing to leave, or to listen to reason. As a last resort, she tried coercion. "Piper, they're going to beat the tar out of us if we don't go now!"

"I guess you shouldn't have done whatever you did that was bad," Piper replied, sounding perfectly casual about it.

This comment pushed Phoebe past worried into downright ticked off. If her big sister wasn't even going to be the least little bit concerned that pink-shirted thugs were threatening to beat them up, then why were they here trying so hard to rescue Piper, when she didn't even really seem to be in any danger?

Of course, the answer to that was that Piper was their sister, and Halliwells stuck together. Unless they couldn't because they were somehow brainwashed, which was the only possible explanation for Piper's behavior. Before she could say anything else to Piper, the security guards grabbed Paige's arm and were reaching past her to Phoebe. "You'll have to come with us," one of them demanded. She was at least eight inches taller than Phoebe, with a tightly drawn platinum ponytail and a glower in her green eyes.

"We have every right to be here," Phoebe protested. "Piper's our sister."

"We're all sisters," the ponytailed one said. She seemed to be the leader, at least of this particular contingent. "You still have to come. You aren't supposed to be here."

"Get your hands off me!" Paige snapped at the two holding her. "This is police brutality!"

"We're not police," another woman said with a sinister smile. Phoebe didn't like the looks of that at all. Three of them had Paige's arms now, and another four had come past her, closing in on Phoebe. Phoebe looked to the women around them for help or support, but none of them—not even Piper—had paused in their workout or paid the least attention to their plight. She tried to weigh their chances of prevailing in a brawl, and decided that while they could possibly do so, they'd have a better chance where there was more room to move and less likelihood that the audience would choose the pink shirts' side over theirs. "Okay," she agreed. "We'll go with you."

"We will?" Paige asked, fixing Phoebe with a *Have you gone insane?* look.

"Yes," Phoebe answered definitively. Paige

shrugged and quit struggling, allowing the security contingent to lead her from the row. Phoebe cast a final glance at Piper, but their sister's gaze was locked on Meg, and she didn't even seem to notice that they were leaving. As they left the row, Meg's pace changed again, quickening into a kind of frenzied dance. The women of the audience changed with her—panting now, sweat flying as they whipped their heads this way and that.

Once they were outside the row, the security women released Phoebe and Paige, but surrounded them in a close formation. The big one in charge said, "This way," and led them toward the front of the arena. At the foot of the stage, they were taken around to the right side, and then behind a hastily constructed fence. From here, Phoebe could just see a sliver of the audience, through the opening in the fence they had entered by, and then even that was blocked off by a wall of pink T-shirts. The tall one with the ponytail stood directly in front of Phoebe and Paige. "You aren't wanted here," she said. "You have come to stir up trouble."

"It's a free country," Paige said flippantly.

The blond woman unfolded her arms, and there was a frightening black automatic pistol in her right hand. "Free country outside," she said, menace dripping in her voice. "Different rules in here."

Chapter
17

Leo sat on grass and scattered needles under a pine tree. He had a view of the canvas panels that surrounded the rally, but he couldn't see inside, and in spite of his best efforts, he couldn't orb in either. He hadn't tried until after Phoebe and Paige had merged with the crowd going in, and now it was too late to let them know.

That worried him more than anything else did. The fact that Meg had magically shielded the rally told him that she had something to hide, even there. Since he couldn't get in, he had to rely on Phoebe and Paige to bring Piper out. He knew there was no one with a better chance to do just that, but as much as he trusted the sisters, he still would have preferred to be in there himself. Since he couldn't be, he waited nearby, just in case he was needed for anything. The day was warm, the sun cheerful, and the smells of pinesap and freshly mowed grass brought him pleasant memories of simpler times. If his wife hadn't been a virtual prisoner, it would have been a nice day.

Even from this distance, he could hear the applause starting, then the music and the stomping. It might sound cheerful to the average listener, but to him it was somehow sinister. He tried not to imagine what might be going on over there, tried to remain alert for any calls for help from Phoebe and Paige even as he blocked out the rest of the din.

But as Leo watched a young father and son tossing a softball around, he saw Darryl Morris, overdressed for the day's warmth in a dark blue suit, his striped necktie knotted tightly at his throat. Darryl looked like he was sweating, but not just from the heat—the expression on his face was worried, nearly frantic. He walked quickly along the perimeter of the canvas panels, as if looking for a way in. *That gives us something in common,* Leo thought, rising from his spot under the tree and dusting off his chinos. With a glance to make sure he was unobserved, he orbed in just behind the police detective. "Darryl!"

Darryl spun around, his hand reflexively shooting toward the holster at his hip. He visibly relaxed when he was Leo. "Leo," he said, "it's good to see you." Then he frowned and ticked his eyes toward the arena. "Does this mean the Halliwells are inside?"

Leo nodded.

"You know what I like?" Darryl asked sarcastically. "I like how when I share information with one of them and ask them to do me the same favor, they never do. That's a good system, don't you think?"

Leo shook his head in sympathy for his friend. "I know exactly how you feel, but that's the way it has to be sometimes."

Darryl nodded sagely. "You, my friend, have the patience of a saint."

"Something like that, anyway," Leo admitted. "What's going on here? Official police business?"

"I have a bad feeling about this whole thing," Darryl told him. "I was trying to find a way in, but they've got it sealed up tighter than a drum."

"You don't know the half of it," Leo said. "Even I can't get in."

Darryl looked at him, surprise registering on his face. "Then things must be worse than I thought."

"That's what I'm afraid of too," Leo agreed.

"Well, I've got a riot squad on the way," Darryl said. "One way or another, we'll get in there."

I hope so, Leo thought. *And I hope we're not too late when we do.*

At the best of times Paige didn't like guns, and she especially didn't like them when they were pointed at her. "You don't need that," she said, aware that her voice squeaked a little with fear.

"Maybe not," said the woman holding it. "But I have it, don't I?"

"No one's arguing with that," Phoebe said. "I'd just like to know why you think you need it."

The woman looked them up and down before answering. "We were warned to watch for you two," she said.

"Warned?" Phoebe asked. "By whom?"

"That's no concern of yours."

"It kind of is," Paige disagreed quickly. *A big concern, in fact.* Had Meg Winship tipped off her security force that they might be here? Or was it Piper—was she really that far gone?

"No," the woman said, shaking her head. "Not anymore. You don't have any concerns anymore."

There was an odd smile on her face, as if she were a mischievous tyke about to do something that would ordinarily get her in trouble, but this time, for some reason, it wouldn't. Paige didn't like it a bit—not the smile, and not the implication of the woman's statement.

Those, combined with the gun in her hand, seemed like real trouble.

Paige looked from one woman to the next, but none of them seemed dismayed by the sight of the weapon, or even the least little bit surprised. "You can't really expect me to believe you're going to shoot us right here," Paige said.

The woman shrugged. "I don't see why not," she said. "It's not like anybody would hear, with that racket."

She had a point there, Paige realized. Between the thundering music and the motion, no one in the audience would be likely to hear a couple of gunshots.

"Phoebe," Paige said, a worried tone in her voice. "I think we should . . ."

She left the sentence unfinished, but Phoebe nodded, anyway.

"Gun," Paige said, trying to orb it from the woman's hand into her own. It didn't come, though. Instead, almost as if she could feel Paige's magical tug, the woman turned and aimed the gun right at Paige's heart.

Phoebe didn't waste another moment. She swept her leg in a half-circle, knocking over the woman closest to her. With the woman off-balance, Phoebe shoved her into the one with the gun.

At the same time, Paige raised her right foot and stomped down onto the instep of the one behind her. The woman let out a grunt of pain and raised her foot off the ground. Paige followed up with an elbow into the woman's jaw, knocking her backward.

The ponytailed one with the gun let loose a shot, but in the chaos of the moment, it went wild and flew over the fence. More hands snatched at Paige, but she kept moving, twisting

from their grasp and striking out with her own
to keep them at bay. She caught a glimpse of
Phoebe in the melee, trying unsuccessfully to
use her levitation powers. Still, Phoebe was a
mistress of the martial arts, and where Paige was
just holding her own, her big sister was kicking
serious butt. She let loose with a snap kick that
caught one of the bigger women in the stomach,
dropping her like a stone, and drove her way
through two others, charging toward the ponytailed one who still brandished the gun.

Paige's strategy would have been different—
she just wanted to run, to get back out into the
main arena, where the sight of a gun might have
had some kind of impact on the brainwashed
drones still working out with Meg. But they
hadn't exactly had a chance to compare battle
plans.

She watched with admiration—in between
fighting off pink shirt–wearing security goons of
her own—as Phoebe waded through the others
like some implacable force. *This would have been
so much easier with witchcraft*, she thought.
*Remind me to vanquish whoever put a magical shield
over this place.* Two of the women grabbed at her
arms, and as she struggled against them, she
saw that three more had collaborated to get hold
of Phoebe. They held her, the biggest one wrap-
ping arms like small tree trunks around her,
as the one with the ponytail leveled her automatic weapon directly at Phoebe's head. Phoebe

fought to free herself, but they held her too tightly. Paige watched in horror as the smirk came back to the ponytailed one's face and her finger tightened on the trigger. She willed herself to orb to the woman's side, but nothing happened.

So she used the more human technique of lashing out with her fists, striking the jaws of the two women who held her. Their grips loosened; Paige dove across the space separating them and smashed into the leader's legs, driving her to the ground. The gun went off with a deafening report, right next to Paige's left ear.

She felt hands on her shoulders and started to bat them away, before she realized they belonged to Phoebe. "Come on, Paige!" Phoebe shouted. "Let's get out of here!" Her voice sounded like it was coming from far away, or maybe underwater, and Paige realized her ear was ringing loudly from the gunshot. But she followed Phoebe's lead, and the two of them dashed back out through the fence, pink-shirted security cadre in close pursuit.

As soon as they broke through the fence and back into the arena, Paige had a flash of insight, something she could see from this vantage point that hadn't been as obvious from within the audience. "Phoebe!" she shouted as they ran.

"What?"

"These women . . . they're not just exercising." She was as certain of her judgment as she had ever been of anything in her life. The women's moves were precise, as choreographed as a ballet. Paige had taken part in similar activities enough times to recognize it for what it was, even though hers usually involved more words and less dance. "They're performing some kind of ritual. And Meg's leading it!"

Phoebe stopped in her tracks, looking from one side to the other. Paige jerked a thumb back over her shoulder. "Phoebes, they're still chasing us!"

"You're right," Phoebe said, her voice filled with awe. "It *is* a ritual! What's she trying to do?"

They started to run again, but the moment had given the security detail a chance to get much closer than Paige found comfortable. "Piper could freeze them all in place and stop it!" she offered. "Except she's part of it!"

"Her powers probably don't work any better in here than ours do," Phoebe added, breathless from the running. "But we've got to do something—whatever Meg's up to, it can't be good!"

Paige felt a sudden impact from behind that forced her to her knees. She tried to turn, but two of the security guards drove into her, pushing her down on the ground, and then more piled on. Phoebe turned to help her, but she was immediately overwhelmed by more, coming from every direction. The women in the audience ignored the sideshow completely, so intent were they on moving in rigid conformity with Meg Winship.

And that, Paige thought as she writhed beneath the press of the women bearing down on her, *is the scariest thing of all.*

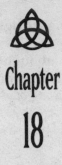

Chapter
18

Leo froze with one fist gripping Darryl's upper arm. "That sounded like a gunshot."

"Maybe," Darryl said, extricating himself from Leo's iron grasp. "There's so much noise from over there, it's hard to tell for sure. But it could have been."

Normally, Darryl knew, a gunshot sounded like nothing else on Earth—people who cringed at cars backfiring did so because that sounded like what they thought a gun might sound. The real sound—the sharp, flat *crack*—was unique, and genuinely terrifying, especially in a crowded urban setting like this one, because it meant someone was in real danger.

"We've got to get in there," Leo insisted.

"I'm with you," Darryl said. The question was, how? He looked around anxiously for the riot squad he had called for, but there was no sign of them. Still, if someone was shooting off a gun behind those canvas walls, he had to get in and do something about it. And he had a gun of his own, with a badge to back it up. Before, he'd been unwilling to force his way through, but now he had every reason to. "Let's go," he said, turning and heading back toward the entrance to the makeshift arena.

The women guarding the way saw him running toward them, this time with another man in tow. They stood up, blocking the entrance with their pink shirt–clad bodies, faces set with sullen determination. "I thought we told you, no men!" one of them shouted as he and Leo approached.

Darryl flashed his badge at the women. "And I told you, I'm a police officer," he declared. "I'm going in."

"No you're not," the seeming leader countered. "Not without a warrant."

"I have reason to believe a crime has been committed in there," Darryl said. "And I'm going inside." He drew back his blazer, both exposing the service weapon in his hip holster and making it readily accessible in case he needed to draw it.

The woman's eyes widened at the sight of it, as if she hadn't really believed that he was a cop—or if she did, she somehow didn't think he'd seriously use the threat of force. She stared at him, then glanced at Leo. For a second, Darryl thought she would challenge Leo too. Instead,

she glanced toward her pink-shirted sisters as if
for support. "You prepared to use that?" she
asked.

Darryl shook his head, barely believing his
own ears. She knew he was a cop, she knew he
had a gun, she knew he suspected that a crime
had been committed, and she still wanted to
play hardball? "Don't need it," he said. He
reached for the handcuffs tucked into the rear of
his belt. "You're under arrest for obstruction of
justice," he said. "The rest of you, either get out
of the way or the same goes for you." Addres-
sing the leader, he added, "Turn around and put
your hands behind your back. I'll read you your
rights later."

She was beginning to do that, her expression
finally beginning to show that she understood
what she had done, when a clamor of screams
erupted from within the walls.

"That's it," Leo stated grimly. He grabbed
Darryl's arm and orbed them around the gate-
keepers. The women who had been in front of
them suddenly reappeared a second later behind
them, astonished looks on their faces. The one
Darryl had been about to handcuff was still in
the process of turning and moving her hands
behind her back. "Come on," Leo said. "My
wife's in there!"

Phoebe had fought multiple opponents before,
and bested them. But those had usually been

demons or other unworldly beasts. These opponents were human, and—dangerous though they might be—she was hesitant about using her most ferocious attacks against them. Anyway, there were about a dozen of them, and they had the advantage of having jumped her while she was running, instead of poised for combat. That shouldn't count—she should always be ready, she knew. But this time she'd been intent on getting Paige out of there, and then distracted by the realization that a ritual was underway—and that Piper was participating in it.

Now she found herself buried under a literal ton of flesh, bone, and muscle—like a quarterback caught by the entire opposing team. She struggled against the weight that crushed her. Her ribs felt like they were on the verge of collapse, and she couldn't catch her breath. And as if that wasn't bad enough, through the melange of bodies piled on her, she could see the ponytailed woman stalking toward her with her gun held close to her thigh and a malevolent glare in her eye.

Then, abruptly, the world went mad.

Though the music continued to blare, Meg Winship halted onstage, and the women in the audience stopped with her. Murmurs of confusion began to spread. Phoebe could only catch the merest glimpse of the stage, but Meg seemed to be frozen in place, her trademark smile now a kind of rictus, artificial and unconvincing.

Even the women holding Phoebe down became aware that something was not right, and their focus shifted enough for Phoebe to gather her strength. With a few well-placed pokes, prods, and kicks, she freed herself from the dog pile. Paige was submerged beneath a similar pile, but the attention of her captors was also on Meg instead of on their prisoner. As Phoebe watched—every bit as caught up in Meg's strange behavior as the rest of the audience— Meg finally broke her paralysis, tilting her head toward the sky and lifting her arms. This time, her fans did not follow suit.

"They come!" Meg shouted, her microphoned voice carrying over the recorded music. Then someone backstage killed the music, and Meg went on without accompaniment. "They're here. The Others grace us with their—"

She froze again. Beside her, on the stage, a shimmering blue circle appeared, warping the air in a pattern like a stone tossed into a clear pool.

That's not good, Phoebe knew. *She's summoned something.*

Which was, of course, the point of the whole ritual, she immediately understood. But a summoning that required such a complex ritual, with hundreds of women in precise motion, wouldn't be necessary for just any low-level demon. No, whatever came through that circle would be something fearsome indeed.

The women in the audience, including the pink-shirted security guards, were now totally consumed by what was happening onstage. Phoebe pushed aside the last couple holding Paige down and took her sister's hand. "Come on," she said quietly. "Things are about to get ugly around here."

Paige laughed. "Like they weren't already?"

"Uglier, then." She tilted her head toward the stage. "Demon time."

As if on cue, the circle of light brightened, becoming a nearly blinding opalescent color, and then a gnarled, clawed hand, with spurs of bone sticking out from its back like thorns on a rosebush, gripped the side of the circle from within, like it was a curtain. The hand was followed by an arm and then a foot, tipped with long, horned claws. All were a putrid yellow-green with brownish speckles. The hand tugged the circle and the rest of the demon emerged. It stood at least eight feet tall, and must have weighed five hundred pounds, Phoebe guessed. The single arm that had come through first was accompanied by two more, giving it a disturbing asymmetry. Its body was corpulent, with rolls of fat undulating with its every motion. Its legs were short and stubby, big around as fire hydrants. And its head—Phoebe didn't even like looking at it, though she was as caught up in it as everyone else—was a jelly-like blob on top of a squat, thick neck, with half a dozen orbs that she thought must have been eyeballs on tiny stalks, and an enormous, slavering maw filled with needle-sharp teeth. When it was fully visible, the blue circle winked from existence.

"Man, that's some seriously heinous dude," Paige whispered in Phoebe's ear. "When you said it was gonna get ugly, you weren't joking."

Phoebe nodded, silent. Meg Winship was in motion again, approaching the horrific thing that now shared the stage with her. "Welcome," she said to it. "I . . . thought there would be more of you."

"There is only one of me," the demon replied, its deep voice oddly soothing. It sounded like some 1940s crooner, and to Phoebe, the contrast between its appearance and its sound only made it that much more awful. "I am all that is needed."

Meg gave the thing a brave smile. "Again, welcome," she said. "These women and I have worked long and hard to bring you through to this plane. You owe us your loyalty, and—"

The demon didn't seem to appreciate that concept. It backhanded Meg with one of those horrible hands, striking her just below the jawline. The bone spurs shredded her skin, blood spurted, and in the utter silence, Phoebe could clearly hear the amplified crack of her neck breaking. She collapsed on the stage, and the demon thumped to the edge of the stage, looking out at the assembled multitude. "What a charming world," it said simply.

As if released from captivity by its words, the women in the audience—the vast majority of them, anyway—began to scream. The ensuing tumult was earsplitting. Now, with Meg's death, they were themselves again. Panic filled the arena. Phoebe could see wild eyes, women turning to those next to them with no idea what they were doing here, some beginning to push or claw at those between them and the exits.

And onstage, the demon, as if unhappy at this response, prepared to climb down into the crowd.

"We've got to do something," Phoebe said to Paige. "And now."

"Piper!" Paige shouted. "Where is she?"

Phoebe stretched to see over the surging mobs, finally catching a glimpse of her sister just a few rows away. She grabbed Paige's hand. "Come on!" She led Paige back toward the stage, like two salmon pushing their way upriver against the tide of bodies that flowed toward the rear.

"Piper!" they both called in unison. After a couple of tries, Piper turned her head and caught Phoebe's eye. She looked momentarily confused, but then smiled as she recognized her sisters.

"Piper, freeze them!" Phoebe commanded. "Everyone."

Understanding washed over Piper's face, and she became an island of calm in the sea of rising terror. She raised her hands, and all around her, the women of the audience froze in place, statue-still.

But the demon didn't freeze. "My subjects!" it cried in dismay, climbing down from the stage. As it did, its obscene bulk rippled like a barely contained vat of gelatin, and once on level ground, it walked toward the nearest of the frozen women.

"Him too!" Paige shouted to Piper. Piper tried again, but the demon didn't stop.

"Okay, blow it up!" Phoebe suggested.

Piper tried that as well, to no avail. "Doesn't work," she said.

Paige tried to orb the creature away, but her attempt was unsuccessful. "I guess we'll just have to kick its enormous butt," Phoebe speculated. She started toward the stage, hands clenched into fists, ready to intercept it. She knew Piper and Paige were following. The thing was huge, and she'd seen how it had dispatched Meg with a casual blow. She had never fought something that looked so physically imposing. *The bigger they are,* she told herself. But even she wasn't convinced.

A moment later, they were close enough for her to smell its hot, fetid breath. She stood directly in front of the demon, blocking it from the frozen audience. Paige moved out to her right, Piper to her left, so if it tried to dodge one, it would run into another. What kind of resistance they could offer, she wasn't sure. But they had to keep it from hurting any of the audience members while they got into position to use the Power of Three.

"You can't be serious," the demon said in its oddly smooth, TV anchorman's voice.

"We may not be as big as you, but we're tough," Phoebe said. "Try us and see."

The thing lashed out at her, moving with unexpected speed and grace for such an ungainly creature. She dodged, but felt the wind from its blow whistle past her, uncomfortably close. When the fist had glided by, she chopped its upper arm with all her strength. Her hand screamed with pain, but the demon barely seemed to notice. Then she had to sidestep because it was bringing one of its arms back for another blow, and she didn't want to let those bone spurs land on her. She leaped into the air, spun, and landed a savage snap-kick. The beast didn't even slow.

This is not going to go well, she thought. *There's no way we can beat this thing physically.*

"Try magic again!" It was Leo's voice, and Phoebe turned to see that he and Darryl were threading their way through the stationary sea of femininity. "Use the Power of Three!"

"What do you think we're doing?" Phoebe answered, scrambling to her feet just before the demon's fist swiped at her. It missed, swiping a few chairs a dozen feet into the air, but another powerful arm drove toward her. She dodged again, unleashing another useless kick, and ran toward her sisters.

Piper and Paige worked their way toward each her quickly. They all knew that when the demon got to the unmoving mob, it would take out its fury on them. Reaching each other, the three sisters clasped hands. Phoebe liked the warmth of Piper's hand in hers, after being apart for so long. "Power of Three," she echoed softly, and she heard her sisters both say the same words under their breaths.

"Any ideas?" Paige asked the others.

"I've got one," Piper replied. As her sister began to speak, Phoebe felt the power within her—the power that was always magnified when the three of them worked together, the power that was greater, as they said, than the sum of its parts—begin to swell.

Horrid beast,
Which here does roam,
Let this spell,
Transport you home!

The demon stopped in its tracks, still just outside striking distance of the nearest group of immobile victims. It let out a plaintive howl that made Phoebe release her sisters' hands so she could cover her own ears, and its pain was palpable. But although they had hurt it, it wasn't yet disappearing, as they had hoped. Phoebe noticed, though, that Paige was in motion too—pitching a vial of the vanquishing potion she had brought with her. Her arm was strong, her aim perfect. The glass vial arced across the bright sky, glittering as it caught the sun.

When it hit the demon squarely, a jet of green flame shot straight into the air like a Roman candle, and a noxious wave of odor, as if the demon's putrescent color had turned to stink, washed across them. "Since we didn't know exactly what we'd be facing," Paige said, "I brought a smorgasbord." She passed out a couple more vials, and each sister took a shot with one. The demon screeched again, blue and red flames joining the green one. Its wail of agony echoed, but when the flame died down, the demon was gone. Phoebe felt Piper reach for her hand again, and she gave it gladly. On the other side, Paige did the same.

"Good throw, Paige," Piper said happily.

"Yeah," Paige agreed. "Not bad at all, if I do say so myself."

"And, I can't help noticing, you do," Phoebe added.

"That's true," Paige said. "I do, don't I?"

The three sisters laughed. Leo, coming up from behind and putting a hand on Phoebe's shoulder and one on his wife's, joined in. After a moment, he spoke. "We're almost done here," he said. "But there is one more thing to take care of. . . ."

Epilogue

Though Piper had only the faintest memory of the last few days, she couldn't deny that it was great to be back at the Manor. She felt as if she'd been gone for months, somehow, like she'd taken a round-the-world cruise without Leo or her sisters—which she would never do—and had only just come home. Everything was familiar, everything was *right*, and she took great comfort in that. Even the plumbing problem at P3 was under control, which she was glad to hear.

The time that she had spent under Meg Winship's sway felt like a half-remembered dream—snatches of it came to her now and again, but she couldn't remember a specific timeline. She could barely even recall Meg's face, and then only from book covers and posters she'd seen around town. Phoebe, Paige, and Leo had filled her in on what had happened, and she believed them, but the whole thing seemed like a story they were telling her, and not an experience that she'd lived through. The only thing she had taken away from it was a renewed sense of her own self-confidence. She felt better about herself, physically and emotionally, than she had in a long time. If that had been an indirect gift from Meg, she was grateful.

Meg's message had been a good one. It had been her methods and her motives that were a problem—summoning a demon was always a bad idea, and Meg hadn't even known what this demon's own goal really was. It had used her, just as she had hypnotized and used her own allies and all the women who had fallen under her spell.

Now they all sat together in the living room at Halliwell Manor, sipping herbal tea and talking over the day's events, and Piper drew satisfaction from simply being in the presence of those she loved more than anything.

"It's a good thing all those women couldn't remember what they saw, when Meg summoned that thing," Paige was saying.

"I can barely remember any of it myself," Piper told them. "If the other women's experiences are like mine, they won't remember much of any of the time they spent under Meg's influence."

"That's probably just as well," Phoebe suggested. "Because if they did remember it, then they'd be much more curious about what happened to Meg. Darryl's official story—neck broken by a falling microphone boom, was it?—might not hold up if they all were to dispute it."

"Yeah, well, I'm not saying it's a bad thing," Paige said. "I wouldn't mind forgetting that ugly guy myself. And his smell, too. You'd think if Meg was going to become a vessel for some nasty, rank demon trying to make his way into our dimension for world domination or whatever, she'd have picked one that was a little more attractive. After all, wasn't she all about the body?"

"Not entirely," Leo countered. "She had a lot to say about the inside too. She tried to improve the whole person, not just the exterior. It really is kind of a shame she was manipulated by that thing."

"And a shame that she manipulated so many of us to bring it here," Piper said. "I don't think I have any ill effects from it, but I did lose a couple of days of my life that I'll never get back."

"Considering what could have happened," Phoebe said, "that's a relatively small price to pay, I think."

"I wish I could forget what happened to Bill," Phoebe said sadly. "Not forget Bill—he was a great guy—but that phone call was awful."

"And it's too bad Dr. Haywood wasn't around for the big event," Paige suggested. "His theory was right after all, I guess. The UFOs were never from outer space—they were just manifestations of the demon's growing influence, in a form that human minds would accept."

"And that would help Meg control our minds," Piper added. "And our bodies, so we could help perform the final ritual." She took a sip from her tea and then stood up and stretched. She'd had enough exercise the last few days to hold her for a month, she figured, but there was only the slightest soreness in her muscles, a minor ache, as if she'd worked out for ten or fifteen minutes too long instead of days. "But you know what I thought was most interesting?"

"What?" Leo asked.

"The women. Meg's victims, I guess you could call them. Us." Piper remembered the faces of the women in the audience—the women who had been, like her, in thrall to Meg Winship's demonically provided magic—after she had unfrozen them. They had turned to one another, confused, uncertain, maybe a little scared to find themselves in an unexpected place, surrounded by strangers. But at the same time, their faces had almost immediately softened. Smiles had blossomed where moments before there had been fear and discomfiture. Women who didn't know one another had started to talk. Piper saw phone numbers being exchanged, hands being held, the timid and scared being comforted by the strong and self-assured. The women didn't even know what they had been through, but they had been through something and had instantly started to bond. Piper heard some of them suggest to others that they work out together, or meet for tea or coffee or lunch on some future occasion. They had made for the exits in an orderly fashion, all panic set aside.

"I think," Piper said, sitting down on the arm of Leo's chair and stroking his shoulder, enjoying the feel of his muscular arm beneath his soft blue sweater, "that instead of being destructive, this demon actually did the city a favor."

"If you don't count Meg," Paige put in.

"Right," Piper agreed. "Not Meg. But in a way, it strengthened us—it brought a thousand women close together, women who otherwise never might have known one another. Even if they never remember what they went through, they now share a bond, and they understand that much. I don't know what they'll do, what they'll accomplish—but whatever it is, it can only be positive. Those women feel good about themselves now, good about one another, and that energy will do good things for us all."

"Which means," Phoebe asserted, "that Meg gets her wish after all. Or part of it, anyway—I guess we'll never know what she was really after, or how much of what happened was her ambition and how much was the demon's."

"We may not be our ideal us," Paige said. "But we're our pretty darn good us—and I'm talking about the collective us, the women of San Francisco. No offense, Leo."

"None taken."

"And pretty darn good is not a bad thing to be."

The sisters laughed again. Piper noticed Leo watching her, love in his eyes, and she leaned over and kissed his warm, slightly stubbly cheek. "Someone needs a shave," she whispered in his ear. "Before, you know, we celebrate my coming home in the proper fashion."

Leo rubbed his face and then stood up suddenly, almost knocking her off the chair. "You're right," he said. "I'll go upstairs and shave. Join me soon?"

"Soon," Piper promised. She wanted to be with her sisters a while longer, just to revel in the joy of being together.

A short while, she thought, with a silent, inner chuckle. She thought of her husband waiting for her in their room.

It's good to be home.

About the Author

Jeff Mariotte is the author of several Angel novels, including *Close to the Ground*, *Hollywood Noir*, *Haunted*, and *Stranger to the Sun*. With Nancy Holder, he wrote the Buffy/Angel crossover trilogy *Unseen* and the Angel novel *Endangered Species*, and with Maryelizabeth Hart added to the mix, the nonfiction *Angel: The Casefiles: Volume 1*. He's published many other books, including original teen horror series Witch Season, original novel *The Slab*, and more comic books than he has time to count, some of which have been nominated for Stoker and International Horror Guild awards. With his wife, the aforementioned Maryelizabeth Hart, and partner Terry Gilman, he co-owns Mysterious Galaxy, a bookstore specializing in science fiction, fantasy, mystery, and horror. He lives in San Diego, California, with his family and pets, in a home filled with books, music, toys, and other examples of American pop culture. More information than you would ever want to know about him is at www.jeffmariotte.com.

As many as 1 in 3 Americans
who have HIV... don't know it.

TAKE CONTROL.
KNOW YOUR STATUS.
GET TESTED.

To learn more about HIV testing,
or get a free guide to HIV and
other sexually transmitted diseases:

www.knowhivaids.org
1-866-344-KNOW